JOHNNY COFFIN
SCHOOL-DAZED

John W Sexton

THE O'BRIEN PRESS
DUBLIN

First published 2002 by The O'Brien Press Ltd,
20 Victoria Road, Dublin 6, Ireland.
Tel: +353 1 4923333; Fax: +353 1 4922777
E-mail: books@obrien.ie
Website: www.obrien.ie
Reprinted 2002.

ISBN: 0-86278-736-X

British Library Cataloguing-in-Publication Data
Sexton, John W., 1958-
Johnny Coffin school-dazed
1.Children's stories
I.Title
823.9'14[J]

2 3 4 5 6 7 8 9 10
02 03 04 05 06 07 08 09 10

The O'Brien Press receives
assistance from

the arts
council
an chomhairle
ealaíon

Editing, typesetting, layout and design: The O'Brien Press Ltd
Author photograph: courtesy Peter Klein
Illustrations: Corrina Askin
Printing: Cox & Wyman Ltd

This book is for
Jenny
who will be no stranger
to such weird happenings
and wayward children

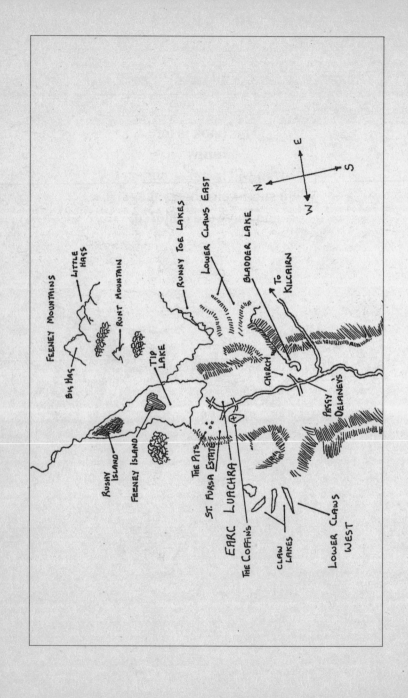

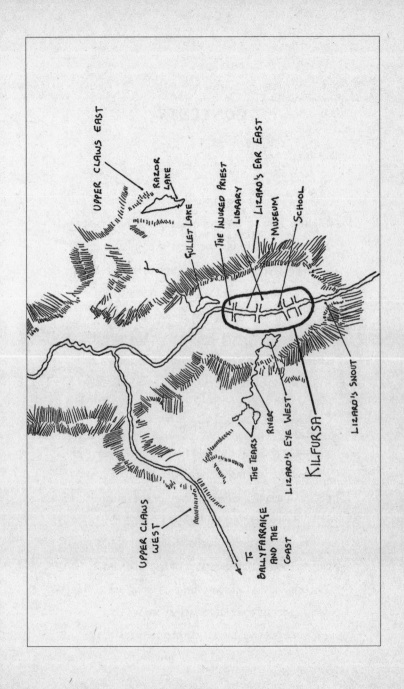

CONTENTS

the fish that took off the arm of our Parish Priest ...

In just enough time that it takes to make a wish, a small shooting star graced the skies above the distant town of Kilfursa. It was twenty-past four in the morning, the first day of May, and Johnny Coffin was standing on the high southern wall of Peggy Delaney's garden. Trying to keep his balance, Johnny held on to a branch of the enormous hawthorn tree that grew up along the inside of the crumbling wall. As his footing became sure he glanced upwards. The shooting star came in that very second.

He'd only ever seen two shooting stars before, and on neither occasion had he remembered to make a wish. But this time he did. Out loud he said: 'I want things to change.'

'What? Did you say something?'

Through the tight, jaggedly barbed branches of the hawthorn tree Johnny could see Enya Murphy walking

along the top of the wall. She was as agile as a cat, even looked a bit like one – her spotty face as flat as a cat's, her ribs ridging her T-shirt.

'I was making a wish,' said Johnny. 'There was a shooting star. Did you see it?'

'Nah, I don't look at the sky. What's the point? The sky's too high, it's never coming down, you might as well forget about it. Me, I never even notice it.'

'Yeah, well, anyway, there was a shooting star, so I made a wish.'

'I hope you wished that this is going to work.'

'Well, I kinda did and I kinda didn't. I just wished that everything would change, which is more or less the same thing. Because if something wasn't happening, then it *might happen* after I wished for things to change.'

'Johnny, you eejit, you just wasted a wish, that's what you did. You should have wished for something specific. At least that way, when the thing you wished for doesn't happen, and it won't, you'd know that making wishes is a complete waste of time. It's even more stupid than looking at the sky.'

Johnny let go of the hawthorn branch and sat down gingerly, his legs astride the wall as if he was riding a horse. He thought: *Wouldn't it be great if the wall started to move away from the garden, himself and Enya on its back. He'd ride the wall up the fourteen-kilometre hilly road to Kilfursa. Then along Main Street they'd go, past all the shops and the post office, bits of the wall falling off as it snaked through the streets, whole chunks of stone falling into shop windows and onto the roofs of cars. People would be running like mad to get out of the way as Johnny would finally bring the wall in through the school gates and to a tar-tearing, grinding stop in the school yard.*

'Johnny! Are you listening to a word? I'm talking to you!' Enya was on the other side of the tree, shaking it like mad, driving its branches towards where Johnny was sitting.

At first, he was not aware of the branches, but of the blood-spotted strips of torn linen that he had tied to the tree on his side. On his side only. Enya had been very particular about that. But why it had to be done on *this* tree, when there were hawthorn trees all over the place, even one in Enya's own back garden, was beyond him.

'Hey, watch it, Enya! You nearly took my eye out!' Then, remembering where he was, he lowered his voice. 'Look, we'd better get out of here. It's not that I'm scared or anything, but you know what they say about Peggy Delaney. And if we wake her up there'll be murder. Anyway, you must have enough of those things by now, and I'm finished over here.'

'I was trying to tell you I had enough. That's what I was saying, you eejit! But you weren't listening; you were miles away. I've got about two cupfuls. That's how much it says you need. I'm getting down.'

13

Johnny couldn't see too clearly because of the tree, but he could make out just enough to see Enya grip a branch with one hand, a plastic bag in the other, and swing out into empty space. She hung in mid-air for the briefest moment, held by her powerful, sinewy arm, then let go. In a second she was on the ground, crouching. She had jumped down from over three metres in height.

'Holy bananas, Enya, you could have killed yourself.'

'Well, I didn't. I'm definitely not dead. But I'm not on the wall either. Come on, Johnny, don't hang about, I'm not waiting forever.'

'Give us a minute, will you? I'm not indestructible like you are.'

'Don't worry,' said Enya, crouching down on the ground, inscribing a circle of fine crystals from a cone-shaped paper bag. 'I've drawn a circle for you out of salt. Brought it for emergencies. Land in that and you'll be perfectly safe.'

'Yeah, right,' said Johnny, no faith in his voice.

He began to ease himself down from the wall, holding on by his arms, his legs blindly below him, his feet scrabbling for a foothold. Finally, his left foot found leverage against a jutting stone, and then his right foot, a bit further down. Still holding to the top of the wall with his arms, then with his hands, he brought his feet down the wall, bit by bit, till his body was almost straight. Then he pushed himself away and made a jump for it. He landed on the ground with a jarring thud, the impact travelling through his entire frame. For a second he steadied, crouch-legged, then lost his balance and fell backwards. He righted himself as quickly as he could and stood up.

Enya was rummaging through the plastic bag. She didn't even bother to look at him as she spoke.

'Yeah, there's enough here, all right. Anyway, are you okay? Try to be more careful the next time. Your arse fell out of the circle. These things make a difference, you know.'

'Yeah, I'm all right, I'm fine. I might have broken every bone in my body, but otherwise, I'm fine. Man, how the hell did you manage to jump like that?'

'I just did it. I suppose if I thought about it I wouldn't have been able to do it, so I didn't think about it. Thinking just stops you doing stuff. Come on, let's get the bikes. I've got to stop in the church on the way. I want to light a candle.'

Johnny watched as Enya scrunched up the plastic bag and stuffed it into the pocket of her fleece, which was hanging from the handlebars of her bike. Then she got on the bike and wheeled it to the road. In a minute she was freewheeling down the hill, a thin siphoning of salt spinning out on her tailwind.

Johnny lifted his bike from the grassy verge where he'd left it. It was wet from the dew-sodden grass. He took a snotty paper hanky from his pocket and wiped

the saddle. Then, letting the tissue fall to the grass, he got on his bike and headed off after Enya.

She never ceased to amaze him. She'd actually managed to drag him out at four o'clock in the morning (he'd had to sneak out the back door) and persuade him to come down to Peggy Delaney's, and take blossoms from Peggy's hawthorn tree and tie those stupid rags on to its branches. It had to be done today, because today was the first of May, and it had to be done early in the morning. That's what the book had said. Well, that's what Enya had said it had said. He hadn't read it himself. She'd told him that she was going to boil the blossoms in rainwater and wash her face with the resultant soup.

'It's for my spots, Johnny. The book says it'll clear them up. It's an old cure. And it's important that you tie these rags to your side of the tree. I can't touch them. It'd take the purging from them. They were pressed against my spots, and each spot of blood on the rags is a spot gone from my face. There's twelve of them now, one for each year of my age. Make sure you don't drop any.'

Johnny always thought it was funny how she wasn't self-conscious around him. She spoke about her spots and all kinds of stuff, wasn't the least embarrassed. Mind you, if somebody else mentioned her spots in her presence, she'd more than likely punch them in the face.

And here she was now, riding down to light a candle in a Catholic church after taking part in some kind of weird pagan ritual. It was hard to make sense of it. Because, as far as he knew, she always refused to go to Mass; her parents couldn't make her do *anything*. Even when she had to go, like when she was in school and had no choice, she would bring along a comic to read. She did it quite openly, was always getting into trouble. And when it came to singing the hymns she'd make up her own words, usually something so funny that everybody near her would be in stitches. But here she was, going down to the church to light a candle. He couldn't figure her out.

Before long he came to the crossroads. Three kilometres ahead was his own village, Earc Luachra, and fourteen kilometres behind him was the town of Kilfursa. And to his right, one kilometre up a tiny road, was the church. The church had been built far outside the village because, apparently, this was the very spot where Saint Fursa had been carried to Heaven. It was a bit of a nuisance, really, because it meant that if you wanted to go to Mass you had to travel four kilometres uphill from the village. Johnny looked up at the small, arrow-shaped sign: CHURCH OF ST FURSA AND THE BLESSED MARY.

At the church gate he parked his bike next to Enya's. He could see that the key was in the church door. Enya had taken it from its hiding place on one of the high,

17

jutting stones in the wall. She was already inside, so he went in through the open door. Screwed to the door was a sign which said: PLEASE KEEP THIS DOOR CLOSED AT ALL TIMES SO THAT BATS AND SWALLOWS DON'T GET INSIDE THE CHURCH.

Johnny went in, closing the door behind him.

Inside the porch, high up on the wall, was a glass case containing a five-foot-long fish, a pike, its mouth fixed with a sinister, razored grin. Johnny stopped to read the polished brass plate underneath the fish. He always stopped to read it, even though he already knew every word by heart. It was just that he found it totally fascinating. He didn't think that there could be any church in the whole world that had a giant fish displayed inside its porch. He was probably right.

On the brass plate was written:

This is the fish that took off the arm of our Parish Priest, Father Enda Murphy, in July 1952. This pike was landed on the shore of Tip Lake, just outside Earc Luachra, two hours after eating Father Enda's arm. It was caught by Paddy Joe Murphy of Earc Luachra West, and was also found to have three Guinness bottles inside its stomach. The Guinness bottles are on display in Kilfursa Museum. This fish has been mounted here in honour of Father Enda by the parishioners of this parish. Late summer 1952.

After reading the plate, Johnny went to the inner door of the porch. It also had a notice about the bats and swallows, in case any forgetful parishioners had left the outer door open. Johnny closed the door firmly behind him.

'Leave the doors open,' called Enya from somewhere ahead of him.

'Ah, Enya, will you give it a break! You're *always* letting the bats in. Last Sunday there were about fifteen of them, flying all over the place, crapping everywhere.'

'Yeah, well, bats have a right to go to church too.'

Johnny ignored her and left the door closed. Light streamed through the east windows, filling the church with a golden glow. The sun was coming up.

Enya was over at the right-hand side of the church, beneath the statue of Our Lady. It looked as if she had lit about thirty candles. And he knew that she hadn't paid for a single one of them. The tiny lights glimmered against the robes of the statue, their indistinct reflections like the souls of moths.

Enya stood between the rows of candles and the statue, her hand inside the mouth of the serpent that was pinned beneath Our Lady's foot. She was following local custom connected to the legend of St Fursa. At school they were told that putting your hand into the mouth of the serpent represented St Fursa's courage when he took on the giant lizard.

'Enya, for crying out loud, how many candles did you light?'

'Thirty-three. Three is my favourite number, and

thirty-three has two threes side by side. Don't they look nice? Here, have you any money?'

Johnny fished inside his pocket and brought out a five-cent coin. He dropped it through the slit in the coin box. The coin hit the bottom of the metal box with a resounding clunk.

'First coin of the day,' said Enya. 'We can owe them the rest.'

'Enya, you already owe Our Lady about a thousand euro.'

Enya looked at Johnny with utter disdain, a gaze of superiority that she was very good at putting on whenever she wanted. 'Johnny, the Blessed Virgin has *no interest* in money. She's only interested in the redemption of souls. She'd be delighted with all these candles. That's why I lit them.'

Johnny said nothing. He knew from experience that it would be a waste of time.

Leaving Enya to her prayers, or whatever it was she was doing, Johnny went over to the alcove to the left of the altar. The sunlight filtered through the stained-glass window of St Fursa and the Lizard. Johnny really loved this window; he had loved looking at it since he was a tiny baby in his mother's arms. The window showed St Fursa, a monk in a brown robe, pulling at the tail of an enormous salamander. As St Fursa pulled at the tail, the very tip was turning to water, and all along the length of the tail right up into the lizard's body, every other part of the lizard was turning to rock and earth. For this was the legend of St Fursa: that he had taken on the last great reptile alive in Ireland, the only one left after St Patrick had banished all the snakes. St Fursa had taken hold of the lizard's tail and had started to pray. It was said that he prayed the Rosary non-stop for seven days and seven nights, all the time keeping hold of the lizard's tail. Because the lizard was so big and St Fursa so small, the reptile wasn't even aware that St Fursa was there. Then, at the end of seven days and seven nights the lizard became sluggish and had to lie down. The tip of its tail turned to water and became Tip Lake, and the rest of its body became the low, stony hills of the surrounding landscape, which stretched in a straight line for over seventeen kilometres, for that was the length of the giant lizard.

After this miracle, the Pope in Rome decreed that St Fursa could have the area of the lizard's dead body as his parish. The village that was built on the shores of Tip Lake was named Earc Luachra, after the Irish name for lizard, and the town that was later built where the lizard's head finally came to rest was named Kilfursa, in honour of the saint himself. Everybody knew that if you looked down at the parish of Kilfursa from an aeroplane, and Johnny had seen it himself, the whole area did, indeed, have the shape of a lizard. Enya, however, didn't put much belief in the legend. She simply thought that Kilfursa's lizard shape was down to the random laws of geography.

Johnny left his musings at the window and returned to Enya. She was still standing at the base of the statue, her hand in the serpent's mouth.

'Enya, do you *have* to do that? It gives me the creeps.'

'Be quiet, will you, I'm saying my prayers. I'm praying that these hawthorn flowers will cure my spots. They've been getting worse and worse for the past few weeks. It's all right for you, you're a boy, and nobody cares if you get spots. But I don't want spots myself. They're ugly.'

Johnny looked at her face. There were angry red eruptions all over her forehead and cheeks. She was covered in them. But the thing was, it didn't really bother him. It's not that he couldn't see them – they were totally unmissable – but it was as if he could see right through them. It didn't seem to make any difference to the look of her face. He still thought she looked great.

'Look, Enya, I've told you before, I don't mind them. Really. But if they bother you, then I hope this hawthorn thing really works. I mean it. That's why I came out here with you. But can you just hurry up? We've got to get back before they miss us at home or Peggy Delaney discovers what we've been up to.

Anyway, I'm dog-tired. I want to get some sleep before I have to go to school. And I haven't even got my homework done. *Again*.'

'I'm nearly finished praying. Just another bit. And, Johnny, I'm glad you came with me. I could probably have done it myself, 'cos I don't need *anybody's help* to do *anything*. But the book said not to touch those rags, and, well, it's kinda lonely doing stuff on your own.'

'Okay. But, look, do you *have* to keep your hand in that snake's mouth – please. It freaks me out.'

'Ah, for God's sake, Johnny, it's not a real snake, it's just a statue.'

'Yeah, but you're still putting your hand inside the mouth of *a snake*.'

'Well, get a grip. There's a bit of a snake in everyone, so why be frightened of them? Look, I bet if you put your hand in *this* one you'd get used to it after a while.'

'Thanks, but no thanks. I'll wait for you outside.'

Johnny walked down the aisle of the church, his shoes crunching on the trail of salt that Enya had let fall from the bag sticking out of her pocket. More than likely she'd leave another line of salt as she followed him down, and he wondered if it was done on purpose. With Enya you could never tell.

Outside, the sun was well risen, bleaching the sky with light. Downhill he sould see the long, shining surface of Tip Lake, with the village on its southern shore. He really wished that Enya would hurry up.

There were still four kilometres to cycle before he'd reach home.

He turned and looked south, up into the green and gold furze-covered hills of Kilfursa. He couldn't see Kilfursa itself, it was too far away, but he knew it was there, the dead head of the lizard, with the school located just about where its brain should be.

At that moment a finch flew past his face, almost brushing him with its wing. He craned his head to watch it. It reached the door just as Enya came out and flew past her into the church. 'I suppose I'd better leave the doors open,' she said, 'just in case that bird wants to come out again.'

Detecting the note of sarcasm in her voice, Johnny thought it best to say nothing. No doubt, by midday the place would be full of birds and the next unfortunate who came to light a candle would have to spend ages shooing them out.

They got on their bikes and cycled down the steep road, the silver waters of Tip Lake beckoning them on.

Batman was up to his knees in the cornflakes ...

A s soon as he woke up, Johnny knew that he shouldn't have gone back to bed. His mother was calling from downstairs to come and get his breakfast – Now! – or he'd miss the school bus. He looked at the clock. He'd never have time to do his homework. Mr McCluskey would go mental.

In the kitchen his nine-year-old brother was sitting at the table playing with a bowl of sodden cornflakes. His eyes were sticky with sleep, a green crust still in the corner of each one. Johnny noticed that a plastic Batman was up to his knees in the cornflakes.

'Mum, Jerry's putting action figures in his cornflakes again!'

'It's not cornflakes, it's quicksand. Batman's got stuck in a swamp and he's gonna get sucked under,' said Jerry.

'It's not a swamp, it's a bowl of cornflakes, you little

dork! And anyway, there's no way Batman's going to drown in cornflakes that only come up to his knees. He'd just wade through them and crawl out over the edge of the bowl. I mean, he's *Batman*. He'd take a bowl of cornflakes in his stride. And wipe the sleep from your eyes, will you, you look totally disgusting.'

Johnny's mother was in the hall, putting lunchboxes into her sons' schoolbags.

'Stop fighting, the pair of you!' she ordered. 'And, Jerry, take Batman out of your cornflakes and eat your breakfast. The bus will be outside any minute.'

Jerry began to knock Batman with the edge of his spoon, pushing him down under the milk. He held Batman there for a few seconds before releasing the spoon. The action figure, being quite heavy, remained beneath the surface of the cereal.

'Batman's drowned,' said Jerry, expressing no emotion whatsoever.

'Yeah, well, I hope you're proud of yourself. There's not many kids who'd want to kill Batman.'

'I didn't kill him. It was this robot spoon. It was made by the Spoonmaster. He's an evil nutcase who wants to rule the world.'

'I know who the nutcase is and it isn't any Spoonmaster. Just wipe your eyes, you little dork,' said Johnny, getting up from the table. All he'd had was a cup of tea and a slice of toast, but he was more concerned about the homework that he hadn't done.

'Hey,' said Jerry, his sharp little brain suddenly inspired, 'have you done your homework?'

'Shut up before I drown you in your cornflakes with Batman, you little turd.'

At that moment the schoolbus pulled up on the main road, its horn giving one single, irritating blare.

Johnny and Jerry ran out to the hall and grabbed their bags.

'See you later, Mum,' Johnny called out as he opened the front door, 'Oh, and check the cornflakes for Batman. There's still a chance he might be alive.'

Out in the street the school bus was belching a thick blue cloud of exhaust. Enya was already on the bus, and so was Snots Murphy. Other kids were there as well, most of them called 'this Murphy' or 'that Murphy' or 'some other Murphy', but Johnny didn't really hang out with that many of them, they just went to the same school. Jerry got on first and sat near the front where all the younger kids went. Johnny made his way down the bus towards the back. He could see Enya standing at the back seat, shoving everybody off. They all left without any complaint, except for Snots, who stayed where he was. Enya sat down next to him.

By the time Johnny got to the back he could see that Snots had a squashed and very dead hedgehog on his lap. He was showing it to Enya, who appeared genuinely fascinated. The stench from the hedgehog hit Johnny as soon as he sat down.

'For crying out loud, Snots, what did you bring that thing in here for? It's gross!'

'I found it on the road just a minute ago. The crows were eating its guts. There's not much left of it except for its bristles. There was this sludgy thing that looked like it could have been its brain lying next to it.'

'Ah man, will you shut up and throw it out the window. I've just had my breakfast.'

'Don't be such a wimp, Johnny,' said Enya, taking the squashed hedgehog from Snots's lap. She held it up before her, as if she was reading a map. A thick, gelatinous streamer of blood hung down from its body.

'Ah, come on lads, this is sick,' complained Johnny, but neither of them was listening. Johnny noticed that everybody else had moved further up the bus.

'Wow, it must be really neat to be covered in prickles,' said Snots. 'I mean, no one could touch you.'

'Yeah, well, fat lot of good it did that little bugger!' replied Johnny, sitting as far over in the seat as he could get, his face turned to the window where a loose seal let in a relieving breeze.

'There's not enough meat left in it for Gristle,' observed Enya.

Gristle Bonehead was Enya's pet crocodile. Gristle sucked up food like a vacuum cleaner and Johnny felt he would be quite happy to accept even a meatless hedgehog. But he said nothing. The hedgehog had suffered enough.

Snots, however, already had plans for the little carcass. 'I was thinking of putting it in Monkey's lunch box. He always brings this enormous lunchbox with about ten sandwiches in it. If we could get to it without him knowing, we could swap his sandwiches for the hedgehog.'

'Brilliant,' said Enya. 'That moron eats like a pig. A squashed hedgehog would make a nice change from ham sandwiches.'

Snots unfastened his schoolbag and pulled out a plastic shopping bag containing his own lunch things. He emptied the plastic bag and stashed his lunch in the pockets of his jacket. Then he held up the plastic bag while Enya dropped in the squashed hedgehog. Holding the bag as far away from himself as possible, Snots expelled all the air and tied the end really tight, then put it into his schoolbag.

'We'll have to look for an opportunity,' said Enya, already fired up with enthusiasm.

Johnny just sat by the window looking out at the passing scenery, thinking about his homework. He considered scribbling something down while on the bus, but even the idea of it tired his brain out. The thing was, he was exhausted from getting up so early in the morning.

'Hey, Enya, did you do that maths homework?' he asked.

'Nah, I'm going to copy mine off Orla Daly. She's not

bad at maths, so my marks'll be quite good.'

'I've done mine, Johnny, if you want to copy it,' volunteered Snots, even though he already knew what the answer would be.

'No thanks, dude. I really appreciate it, but most of your answers will be wrong, 'cos maths is about the only subject you're no good at. McCluskey will take great delight in asking me how I arrived at this answer and that answer and how *extraordinary* it is that Mr Coughlan's wrong answers are the same as Mr Murphy's wrong answers. Then we'll both get detention 'cos he'll rumble that you let me copy from you. Anyway, I'm not really into copying. I just wondered if Enya had done it, that's all. If she hadn't, then we would have been in detention together. I mean, detention with Enya is a laugh.'

Enya said nothing. She seemed to be in a world of her own, staring out of the other window, occasionally scratching at one of her spots. Johnny noticed that the spots were all present and correct. The rag cure and the prayers obviously hadn't kicked in yet.

The bus went on, spreading its blue exhaust up the hilly roads to Kilfursa. Soon it came into Kilfursa Town and eventually reached the gates of Saint Fursa Combined School.

Johnny, Enya and Snots were the last to leave the bus, but they didn't follow the others in through the school gates. Instead they made their way back down the main street. They were going to call on Jimmy Pats Murphy, whose parents ran one of the local pubs. This was their usual morning ritual. After collecting Jimmy Pats, they'd all walk back to the school and slouch through the gates just before the bell rang.

Halfway down the main street they came to the pub, The Injured Priest. As usual, the front door was open and they walked in. Jimmy Pats's father was sweeping the floor of the lounge and he wished them a half-hearted good morning. While they waited for Jimmy Pats, they went up to one of the walls where there was a glass display case. Although they saw it every school morning, they never tired of its contents. Indeed, the contents of that display case were one of the treasures of Kilfursa, and possibly the main tourist attraction of the entire town.

Inside the case was the preserved left arm of Father Enda Murphy. After being embalmed, presumably as a mark of respect and good taste, Father Enda's arm had been dressed in a white shirt-sleeve with a silver cuff-link. Some of the locals complained that a silver cuff-link wasn't becoming of a priest, but Jimmy Pats's father said that they were only begrudgers. Beneath the case was a brass plate with an inscription:

This display case contains the left arm of Father Enda Murphy, first cousin of Tim Mike Murphy, the original proprietor of this public house. Father Murphy lost his arm in an accident in July 1952 while fishing on the waters of

Tip Lake. His arm was later retrieved by Tim Mike's brother Paddy Joe, who pulled it from the stomach of a giant pike. Also inside the pike's stomach were three Guinness bottles, which can be seen in Kilfursa Museum.

Johnny often wondered about those three Guinness bottles. He wasn't too curious as to why the pike had swallowed them, but he always thought it was strange that the bottles were on display in the museum. As far as he was concerned, the bottles should have been on display in the pub, the arm should have been on display in the church, and the fish should have been on display in the museum. To him the whole thing was organised backwards, but nobody could give him a satisfactory answer as to how it had come about. His Dad said that it was just the way it had been done. You obviously had to be an adult to understand it.

After a few minutes, Jimmy Pats came down with his schoolbag and they left the pub and made their way back to the school.

Only one of the school gates was open and they had to step over the principal's dog, a heavily muscled Boxer called Vigrid, who was fast asleep in the narrowed opening. As they crossed over him, one by one, the dog's guts rumbled beneath them like a living engine. For a moment, Johnny wondered if Vigrid had been there when Jerry had gone into the school earlier. Johnny knew that if that was the case, then Jerry would have got into the yard by climbing over the gate. Jerry was scared of his life of dogs, and Vigrid simply terrified him.

Inside the school yard Orla Daly had two boys in a headlock, one under each arm, and was extremely annoyed when Enya disturbed her to ask for the maths homework. But Orla wasn't going to argue with Enya, because Enya was even tougher than she was. Still, she wasn't at all pleased that she had to let the boys go. They slunk off, one nursing a bloody nose, the other a reddened ear, without either of them thanking Enya for her intervention.

While Enya copied Orla's homework, Johnny sat on the grass verge feeling totally depressed. Mr McCluskey would do his nut. That was certain. And he'd humiliate Johnny in front of everyone. That was another certainty. Oh man, why did his life have to be such a mess? At that moment the bell rang for the start of school.

his face was completely covered in warts ...

Saint Fursa Combined School had its own special charter. It was, in fact, two schools, a secondary and a primary, both sharing the one enormous complex of buildings. The pupils in the final two years of the primary were taught certain subjects that would normally be found only in secondary schools in other parts of the country, but this was to facilitate the transition to the secondary part of the school. It was a tradition peculiar to Saint Fursa's.

The head of the entire combined school was Mr Chamberdale, and the head of the primary section was Johnny's class teacher, Mr McCluskey. McCluskey could be a bit of a pain, especially if you didn't do your homework, but it was Mr Chamberdale whom Johnny found truly frightening. It was nothing to do with the man's behaviour; it simply stemmed from the way he looked.

Mr Chamberdale was tall and bald, and his face was completely covered in warts, obviously due to some strange medical condition. His eyes were pale blue and sad, and he had square, brown teeth that jutted out when he spoke. Luckily for Johnny, he had never had any dealings with Mr Chamberdale. Nevertheless, whenever they passed each other in the corridor, Johnny always avoided his gaze and Mr Chamberdale seemed not even to notice his presence.

And that was the funny thing. Because this morning things seemed different.

'I'm telling you, Johnny, Chamberdale was definitely looking at you. He was staring directly at you,' Snots Murphy observed.

'Nah, you were definitely imagining it, Snots,' said Johnny, unnerved nevertheless, as they filed into Mr McCluskey's classroom.

The first lesson was maths. Mr McCluskey ordered everybody to get out their homework and Johnny went through the motions of pulling out books. At that moment there was a knock on the door and a prefect from the upper years came in. The prefect handed a note to Mr McCluskey and then left. Mr McCluskey unfolded the piece of paper and began to read.

As he read, there was total silence. Mr McCluskey lifted his head from the note for a moment, looked out the window into the distance, then returned to the piece of paper. The truth was, there were only six words

35

written there, but Mr McCluskey knew that the very arrival of the note in the room had sent a shiver of expectation through the entire class. He milked it for all it was worth. He folded the note, put it on the palm of his left hand and began to tap it with two fingers of his right hand, as if considering a great decision. Then he got up from his desk and began to pace back and forth in front of the blackboard. Finally, he looked directly at the class, but focused on no one in particular. Everybody held their breath, except for Enya, who was genuinely fearless and therefore unimpressed.

'Coughlan!' screamed Mr McCluskey suddenly, his voice brittle with accusation.

'What? *Me*, sir?' said Johnny, taken by surprise.

'Yes, you, Coughlan. Have you done something, Coughlan?'

'D ... done something, sir?' Johnny was genuinely confused. He looked at Mr McCluskey but the teacher's thoughts were impenetrable. Then it dawned on him. This had nothing to do with the note. This was one of McCluskey's tricks. In fact, Johnny was now quite certain that the note had nothing to do with the class at all. McCluskey had just done all that pacing to manipulate their fears. He was always doing that kind of thing.

Johnny straightened up. He wasn't going to let McCluskey fluster him.

'Oh, you mean, have I done *the homework*, sir? Just give me a minute, sir; it's in my bag here somewhere, sir. I'll have it in a second, Mr McCluskey.' Yes, Johnny had decided to bluff.

'*Homework*, Coughlan?' screamed Mr McCluskey.

'Yes, sir, I'll have it in a second, sir,' said Johnny with genuine confidence. He was beginning to feel pleased with himself. He was taking control of the situation.

'I'm not talking about homework, Coughlan. I'm talking about this note, boy.' Mr McCluskey held up the neatly folded square of paper, his voice triumphant.

Johnny looked at him, dumbfounded. Everybody in the class looked at Johnny, especially Enya, who was envious that he could be in so much trouble. To Enya, trouble was good fun; she went out of her way to court it.

'I don't understand, sir,' said Johnny, his face reddening, his legs beginning to shake.

'Well, Coughlan, according to this note, Mr Chamberdale wants to see you immediately. *Immediately*, Coughlan. And you can take the note with you.'

Johnny went to the front of the class and took the note. Out in the corridor he opened it up, hoping for a clue; hoping, perhaps, to discover that it was nothing at all.

The note said: *Send Coughlan to my office. Now.*

He was the only Coughlan in the class, so there was

no chance of a mistake. Johnny looked at the word *Now*. He had not realised how horrible a word it was until that very second. It snapped its meaning from the folded paper without any nonsense. Johnny knew it meant trouble. But he had no idea what he could possibly have done.

He left the primary-school section and entered into the larger part of the school. Along the way he met Vigrid the dog. Vigrid glanced at him but only for a moment, a glance displaying little interest, and then walked past him in the opposite direction. Mr Chamberdale's dog wandered the school all day long, could end up *anywhere*, and was usually spotted almost *everywhere*. He even went into the classrooms and would sit through entire lessons, fast asleep beneath the blackboard. But none of the teachers seemed to mind as everybody was used to it. Johnny followed the dog with his gaze until he turned a corner and was out of sight.

Johnny wasn't quite sure where the principal's office was and seriously considered getting lost. An hour's aimless wandering – that would just about do it. He could be like Vigrid, traipsing throughout the school without any intent whatsoever. Then he came to a sign. It said: Principal's Office, Second Floor, with an arrow that pointed up the stairs. Johnny sighed and began to climb the stairs, his legs becoming leaden with fear, his stomach jittering crazily.

When he came to the office there was already somebody sitting outside. A fourteen-year-old student whom everybody knew by reputation, because his reputation wasn't very good. He was a big brute of a kid called Raymond Murphy. He had hands that looked as if they could break coconuts. His hair was brown and wavy, and his eyes were black and shining. He looked at Johnny with belligerence and then amusement.

'Are you waiting to go next?' asked Johnny, feebly.

Raymond waited a moment before answering, a very long moment, pretending that he hadn't heard. But then he seemed to have a change of heart and said: 'I've already seen him. He told me to wait here until he called me again. He's working out what to do. He always does that. Just knock on the door and wait for him to answer. You'll have to knock about three times before he calls you in.'

Johnny knocked on the door and waited, but there was no reply. He waited a few more moments and knocked again, this time much louder, but still there was no reply. Raymond Murphy just sat there, grinning. He was obviously well-accustomed to the ritual. Johnny knocked a third time and Mr Chamberdale called him in.

As Johnny stepped into the principal's office he noticed that it was dark. The blinds were closed and the only light came from a green-shaded lamp on the huge desk. Johnny thought that he could hear a sound like laboured breathing, something like an undercurrent that ran through the room.

Mr Chamberdale sat at his desk, writing in a ledger. When Johnny approached the desk, the principal looked up. He put down his pen and picked up a pair of tweezers. Johnny felt a strange sensation move through his gut. The tweezers shone in the light from the desk-lamp.

'Well. Coughlan, is it?' said Mr Chamberdale, turning the tweezers in his hand.

'Yes, sir,' said Johnny, not daring to take his eyes off the tweezers.

'Have an early start this morning, did you, Coughlan?' said Mr Chamberdale.

'Er ... excuse me, sir?' said Johnny.

'Got up bright and early, did you, Coughlan?'

So that was it! They had been found out already. At that moment Johnny hated Enya. She was a nutcase, that's what she was. Her and her hair-brained schemes. Then he snapped out of it. Johnny looked straight into Mr Chamberdale's eyes; they seemed to pierce right through to Johnny's brain.

'Yes, I do get up early, sir,' said Johnny, feebly.

'So I hear,' said Chamberdale, opening a drawer in his desk and reaching in with the tweezers. Johnny had no idea what was going to happen next. But he had a feeling that he would not like it.

As Mr Chamberdale's hand came out of the desk, Johnny saw that he had picked something up with the tips of the tweezers. He placed it in the centre of his desk. It was a soggy, snot-encrusted paper tissue. Johnny looked at it in disbelief.

'I believe this is your property, Coughlan,' said Mr Chamberdale. 'It was brought in to me by Peggy Delaney of Kilfursa East, first thing this morning. She says you left it behind you, after wiping the saddle of your bicycle. She also says that she was awoken at an ungodly hour this morning by some pair bickering on her garden wall, and that she saw *you* quite plainly. Unfortunately, she couldn't make out your accomplice as he was hidden behind the branches of a hawthorn tree. Perhaps you could tell me who you were with and what you were doing there, Coughlan?'

Johnny looked at the sodden tissue. He stared at it as if it was the most wonderful thing in the world. He did this because the alternative would have been to look into Mr Chamberdale's face.

In the silence, the breathing sound seemed to become louder and louder. As Johnny looked up, he realised for the first time where the noise was coming from. It sounded like breathing because it *was* breathing. It was coming from the corner of the room, where Vigrid was lying with his head in his paws, his eyes two glowing slits. The slits were looking at Johnny.

Johnny gazed at Vigrid with his mouth open, wondering how the hell the boxer could have got into Chamberdale's office when he had only just seen him in the corridor a few minutes earlier, going slowly in the opposite direction. *Definitely* going in the opposite direction.

'I'm waiting, Coughlan,' said Mr Chamberdale.

Johnny looked back at the principal and the dog suddenly left his thoughts. He was well and truly caught. But there was no way he could say what he was doing on Peggy Delaney's wall without betraying Enya.

'I'm sorry, sir, but I can't tell you who was with me, sir. It was a friend, sir.'

Mr Chamberdale sat back in his chair. From his place in the corner Vigrid snorted.

'I see, Coughlan. A friend, was it? Well, we'll find out who your friends are and we'll just put two and two together, won't we? And let me tell you, Coughlan, I'll find out before the day is up. Go back to your class, Coughlan, and take your dirty handkerchief with you.'

Johnny picked up the tissue and suddenly felt ridiculous.

'Now, Coughlan, give this note to Mr McCluskey. And don't read it.'

Johnny hesitated at the door and turned to look at the dog.

'Well, is there something else, Coughlan?' asked Mr Chamberdale, a hint of impatience entering his voice.

'Excuse me, sir, it's about your dog, sir.'

'What about him, Coughlan?'

'Er, why is he called Vigrid, sir? Is he named after somebody?'

'Vigrid is the name of a place,' replied the principal, who was now writing once more in his ledger.

Johnny hovered at the door. That was the weirdest thing he'd ever heard. Why would anybody want to name a dog after a *place*?'

'Er, was he born there, sir?' asked Johnny, suddenly convinced that he'd discovered the answer.

'No, Coughlan. Vigrid is a place in Scandinavian mythology. It's where the final battle is to be fought between the gods, where all of creation eventually comes to an end. It is a place of such unspeakable violence that it seemed an appropriate name for a Boxer dog. But as you can see, he doesn't live up to his name. Now, Coughlan, stop wasting time and get back to your class.'

On the way down the stairs Johnny opened the note that Mr Chamberdale had given him for Mr McCluskey. It said: *Golf? Four o'clock?*

When he got back to his class, Johnny noticed that his schoolbag was missing from his desk. Mr McCluskey was asking Julie Hegarty to explain one of her answers to the homework. Johnny looked around frantically for his bag. He caught Monkey Murphy's eye. Monkey grinned maliciously, leaned forward in

his desk, and passed his finger across his throat with a cutting motion. It was obvious that Monkey knew where Johnny's bag was. Then Johnny looked over at Enya, and he saw her pointing with her eyes to the front of the class. Johnny looked up to see his schoolbag on Mr McCluskey's desk, and all his books spilt out. On the very top of his pile of books, opened on the last page, was Johnny's maths copybook. This wasn't good.

Johnny sat through the next few minutes in a panic. He was rumbled. He knew McCluskey had caught him out, had discovered that he hadn't done the homework. The best he could hope for was that McCluskey would keep him back until the end of the lesson and not humiliate him in front of the class. Unfortunately for Johnny, the best he could hope for wasn't going to happen.

'What's wrong, Coughlan? Are you looking for something, boy?'

'It's my bag, sir. I see it on your desk, sir.'

'Oh yes, Coughlan. No doubt you were looking for your maths copybook. The maths copybook with the maths homework in it.'

'I didn't do the maths homework, sir. I was bluffing, sir.'

Mr McCluskey came up to Johnny's desk and stood over him. He looked disappointed, and Johnny realised why. By simply admitting straight out that he hadn't done the homework, Johnny had deprived Mr McCluskey of his usual sport.

'Bluffing, were you, Coughlan? And let's see, now, is there anybody else in the class who's been bluffing? Is there anybody else who hasn't done their homework?'

For a moment there was no response. Then Enya put up her hand. Johnny was stunned. He knew that Enya had copied Orla's homework and that if she'd simply said nothing she would have got away with it. It seemed totally stupid that she had just owned up to not doing it. He couldn't work it out.

'Miss Murphy, I see,' said Mr McCluskey. 'Well, the pair of you can see me for detention on Thursday at lunchtime.'

Johnny sat back in his chair and breathed a sigh of relief. It wasn't too bad after all. At least he'd be in detention with Enya. That'd be a laugh. She was a star. He felt a moment of guilt for the nasty thought he'd had about her in Mr Chamberdale's office, but the moment quickly passed.

Mr McCluskey was looking at Johnny. Somehow Johnny could tell that Mr McCluskey knew he'd been cheated. But he made Johnny pay for it for the remainder of the lesson, badgering him with maths questions for a full half-hour.

more police cars than there's police ...

At first break Johnny told Enya, Snots and Jimmy Pats about his visit to Chamberdale. Enya seemed impressed that he hadn't given her away. But Johnny was still worried about what would happen next. And what about the rest of it? Surely Peggy Delaney hadn't just complained about the hanky? But he couldn't mention the rags in front of Jimmy Pats and Snots. They knew nothing about it.

Enya had more pressing business on her mind: the matter of the dead hedgehog in Snots's schoolbag.

'Listen,' said Enya, 'we've got to get it into Monkey's schoolbag without him noticing. The problem is he has the bag with him at all times 'cos that's where he keeps his cigarettes and all the stuff he's not supposed to have and that he doesn't want people to steal. We'll need a distraction, and we'll have to do it now, otherwise we'll never get the thing in his lunchbox before lunchtime.'

It was decided that Johnny would be the decoy, mainly because he refused point-blank to actually handle the hedgehog. Monkey and Orla were sitting together on the school steps when Johnny approached them. His intention was just to engage in smalltalk, so he said the first thing that came into his head.

'Hey, lads, do you know what I saw this morning? A shooting star. It must have fallen somewhere near here. Probably a meteorite.'

Monkey leant forward. Usually he didn't have much time for Johnny, but for some reason he seemed full of enthusiam.

'Nah, that wasn't a meteorite, that was a UFO. They've been landing north of Kilfursa since last Wednesday morning. People reckon one came down near where Mr McCluskey lives, out in Lizard's Snout.'

'Yeah, right,' said Johnny, suddenly becoming suspicious that Monkey might be winding him up. 'How come there aren't aliens running about all over the place so?'

'How do ya know there aren't?' said Monkey. 'Anyway, what would you know about it, Coffin? You live down there in the Lizard's arse, miles away. You just don't know what's going on up here. I mean, there's been police cars up and down the roads for the past few nights. More police cars than there's police in Kilfursa. They must be bringing police in from all over the country.'

47

'Look,' said Johnny, suddenly feeling contentious, 'if there were UFOs landing up here, then they'd be sending in the army, not the police.'

'Who's to say?' said Monkey. 'If refugees smuggled themselves in from Russia then the police would come in, not the army. Maybe aliens from outer space are considered the same as refugees. How the hell would I know? All I know for certain is that there's definitely *something* going on.'

'And those things coming down aren't meteorites,' said Orla, "cos if they were the whole place would be full of impact craters, but there's nothing like that either. I reckon it's UFOs, but it's nothing stupid like you see in films. It's something else.'

'Yeah, like what?'

'I don't know. I'm just saying that it's not meteorites and that the police are taking an interest in the whole thing.'

Johnny was finding this interesting, and wanted to know more, but at that moment, just as they had planned, Enya came down the steps from behind and sat between Monkey and Orla.

'Look, Orla, thanks for letting me cog from your homework. I really appreciated it.'

'Yeah, so how come you told McCluskey you hadn't done it? Seems like a waste to me.'

'Ah, you know, it was just the idea of Johnny doing the detention on his own.'

Johnny could see Snots coming down the steps behind them. He grabbed Monkey's school bag and walked back up the steps with it. No one turned round.

'Oh yeah, and another thing,' said Monkey, 'about those shooting star things. Seamus Murphy reckons he actually saw one land in his back garden.'

'Seamus Murphy?' said Enya. 'The same Seamus Murphy who swears that the ghost of Elvis Presley played 'Heartbreak Hotel' at his Grandad's funeral, and that everybody saw it, even the priest? Seamus is a born liar. He couldn't tell you his correct name if you asked him.'

'I know that,' said Monkey. 'Like, I'm not an idiot. But the thing is, it's not just that he says it landed in his garden, it's what he says it *did*. He says this big ball of hot glass, the size of a fridge, came down in his garden and then suddenly turned into light. And it just passed into the ground without making a mark. Now, that's the same as what Orla said about these shooting stars not leaving any craters.'

'I don't know, Monkey,' said Johnny. 'I mean, Seamus has this really vivid imagination. I mean, his description of Elvis was brilliant, but it was still a lie.'

At that moment Johnny could see Snots coming back down the steps with Monkey's bag. He put it down where he had got it, then he walked past them, as if he was just coming down for the first time.

'Hey, what's going on?' asked Snots.

'Nothing we'd want to tell you about, you little cretin,' said Monkey.

'Look,' said Johnny, 'don't be picking on him. He was just asking.'

Monkey leaned back against his bag, and Johnny was glad that he hadn't done that sooner.

'So, Coffin, what happened with Chamberdale?' asked Monkey.

Johnny saw the question as the perfect opportunity to sow a little misinformation, something that could be used to throw Monkey off the scent later.

'He's seeing me later today; he hasn't made up his mind what he's going do about me. Someone was telling lies about me and he's going to check them out. Anyway, it wasn't too bad, 'cos Raymond Murphy – you know, that big gorilla in the secondary school – anyway, he was before me and he seemed to be in so much trouble that Chamberdale wasn't really bothered with me.'

'Raymond Murphy's a complete nutcase,' said Orla. 'He's always getting himself into trouble. He's even worse than Enya here.' She nudged Enya and began to laugh.

'So, what had he done?' asked Monkey.

'I don't know,' said Johnny. 'I heard Chamberdale say something about a hedgehog.'

'A hedgehog?'

'Yeah. Apparently Raymond had been seen carrying a dead hedgehog around the school with him, and Chamberdale wanted to know where it was now. Something to do with health and safety. But I didn't really hear that much, so I don't know any more than that.'

As Johnny finished, the bell rang for the next lesson.

a cure for reeking armpits ...

Later in the day a prefect came into the class and handed Mr McCluskey a note. This time he read it without any fuss.

'Coughlan and Enya Murphy, Mr Chamberdale has decided that he wants to see you both straight away. Go to his office at once.'

Everyone stared at them as they left the room, but out in the corridor Enya was over the moon with delight.

'This is great. We're missing that stupid lesson. Okay, you've been there before, Johnny, so you'd better lead the way.'

Once at Mr Chamberdale's office, Johnny knocked at the door. There was no reply, so he knocked a second time, and then a third. Mr Chamberdale called them in.

'Ah yes, Johnny Coughlan from Earc Luachra. And you must be Enya Murphy.'

Mr Chamberdale looked Enya up and down.

'Well, young lady, you look as if you could scale a three-metre wall.'

'With my eyes closed, sir.'

Oh God, thought Johnny, *this is going to be a complete disaster. She'll say something smart and we'll be expelled from the school.*

'I hope you realise that climbing into people's gardens at four-thirty in the morning is a very serious business. I'm trying to decide who I should inform first, your parents or the police.'

Johnny swallowed. This was not going very well. In fact, this *was* going to be a complete disaster.

'Well, actually, sir,' said Enya, and Johnny was thinking: *Please, please, don't say another word, you'll only make things worse*, 'we didn't *actually* climb into anybody's garden. We just happened to be on top of Peggy Delaney's wall because she has a hawthorn tree, and we needed the blossoms.'

Mr Chamberdale sat back in his chair, his blue eyes wide open, their customary sadness replaced by curiosity.

'You see, sir,' continued Enya, 'we had to be there so early in the morning because that's the tradition, sir. And we had to do it today because today is the start of May and that's the best time to pick them, sir. You see, you make a kind of soup out of them and you wash your face in it. It's for my spots, sir. Johnny was helping me, sir, 'cos he's my boyfriend. Look, I'll prove it to you.'

From the pocket of her fleece Enya pulled out a well-thumbed paperback book. On the cover was the title: *Folk Medicine*. She passed it across the desk and turned it so it would be the right way up for Mr Chamberdale to read.

'So, sir, you can see why we had to be discreet. Telling people what we were doing would just be too embarrassing.'

Mr Chamberdale looked through the book. He found the page concerning the hawthorn blossom marked with a scruffy bookmark. He read to himself for a few minutes while Johnny and Enya waited in silence. Then he leafed through the rest of the book: a cure for backache; a cure for bad breath; a cure for reeking armpits; a cure for flatulence; finally, Mr Chamberdale came to a cure for warts. He tried to memorise the required ingredients and even considered confiscating the book, when he became aware of the two misfits staring at him. Eventually he looked at Johnny.

'Well, Mr Coughlan, this seems to change things. I now see that your refusal to explain yourself was really quite noble. You were trying to protect your girlfriend from embarrassment. Very commendable. However, there is still the matter of an apology for scaring the wits out of Peggy Delaney. You should attend to that as soon as possible. Next weekend is the May bank-holiday weekend, and I suggest you think of something you can do to make amends before then. I'll be phoning her myself in the meantime, to explain what you were doing. Now, I'm letting you off, but only because I'm satisfied that nothing malicious was going on. And make sure you don't ever come before me again. Now, take this note and return to your class.'

On the way down the stairs, Johnny's head was in a spin. 'Hey, Enya, did ya hear what he said?'

'Yeah, he said he was letting us off. Well, why shouldn't he?'

'No, no, you don't get it. He said, "this seems to change things."'

'You're right. I still don't get it. What the hell are you talking about?'

'That's what I wished for when I saw that shooting star. Remember? I wished that things would change. And look what happened. Chamberdale and McCluskey both caught me out, but instead of turning out badly it turned out for the best. That's a change, isn't it? We should have been in dead trouble, but because of my wish, things weren't so bad, after all. Don't you get what this means? Now I'll be practically indestructible. I'll be able to do anything I want. I'll be protected by that wish I made, because I'll no longer have to expect all the bad results that I'm used to.'

'Oh, right. So why are we walking down the stairs, then? If you're so indestructible why didn't you just jump from the window of Chamberdale's office? Look, Johnny, if I bite you on the ear then it'll bleed. This stuff about change is crazy talk. I told you before, wishes don't come true. I don't know how many times I've wished for these spots to go. You have to *do* stuff to make things happen, Johnny. Take my word for it.'

But Johnny couldn't take her word for it. It was as if there was a fever in his brain. He was suddenly convinced that what he believed was true. *I'm invincible*, he kept thinking to himself. *Invincible, invincible*.

'Anyway,' said Enya, 'you're forgetting something. Chamberdale never mentioned the rags. Which means Peggy never told him about them. And if Peggy never told him about them, then that means she's gonna do something about them herself.'

But Johnny wasn't really listening. The rags didn't mean that much to him. He just didn't get it. And Enya knew that. But she also knew that he'd get it soon enough. He'd soon discover that Chamberdale was

nothing compared to Peggy Delaney.

At the bottom of the stairs they bumped into Raymond Murphy, on his way up.

'Hey,' said Johnny. 'I had to go to see Chamberdale again. He let me off. This is my girlfriend, Enya.'

The big lout looked down at them as if they were insects. 'Yeah, sure you did. Listen, Chamberdale never lets *anyone* off. Never. I should know. He's never let me off once in three years, and I see him every week. Amn't I seeing him for the second time today?'

As Raymond pushed his way past them, going up the stairs, Johnny was convinced this was the proof he was looking for.

'Did you hear what he said? *Chamberdale never lets anyone off*. I'm telling you, it's that wish I made. Things are going to change.'

Just as they reached the classroom door Johnny remembered the note that he'd been given for Mr McCluskey. It contained only three words: *No action necessary*.

While they went to their desks, Mr McCluskey read the note. They watched as he read it several times. An expression of intense puzzlement seemed to descend on his face. Finally, he put the note in his top pocket and rose up from his desk. Johnny waited for some sarcastic remark, but none was forthcoming. Not once through the remainder of the lesson did Mr McCluskey ask a single question of Johnny or Enya. In fact, he seemed to be going out of his way to ignore them.

'I'm invincible, invincible, invincible,' muttered Johnny under his breath.

Johnny decided to conduct an experiment. He put his head down on his desk and fell asleep. Ten minutes later he woke up. McCluskey was still blathering on about something or other; he hadn't noticed at all. Johnny opened his schoolbag and took out a comic. He placed it on the desk and read it quite openly. McCluskey just droned on and on. And on.

'I'm invincible, invincible,' muttered Johnny. '*Invincible.*'

After the lesson Johnny walked out of the class with the comic under his arm and his lunchbox on his head. McCluskey didn't say a thing.

As Johnny looked back over his shoulder, he saw Mr McCluskey begin to clean the blackboard. Motes of chalkdust were filling the front of the classroom. They were lit up by the sunlight slicing in through the window and seemed to surround the teacher in a wonderful, sparkling cloud. It was as if McCluskey had somehow been defused. He looked like somebody's nice uncle out of a fairytale.

Yeah, thought Johnny, *things have definitely changed*.

the squashed hedgehog was some kind of puppet ...

During lunchbreak, Johnny and the gang made sure that they were as close to Monkey as they could possibly get without making it look obvious.

He was sitting back on the steps again, the lowest ones this time, one of his favourite spots, and Orla was with him. Monkey was rabbiting on about something and Orla looked totally bored. Vigrid was there as well, looking content as Monkey massaged his fingers into the top of Vigrid's head. Monkey was one of the few pupils in the school that the dog would allow to touch him. For some reason Monkey got on very well with dogs. He was definitely a dog person.

Orla was stifling a yawn as Monkey went on and on about whatever it was he was going on about. Orla had no idea what he was saying because she wasn't really listening. As Monkey withdrew his hand from Vigrid's head, Vigrid took a step sideways and began to shake his body vigorously, his muscles magnificent as he sent them wobbling in that mad, brisk tremble that dogs do best.

After loosening himself up, Vigrid ambled off.

Still gabbing on and on to an unattentive Orla, Monkey began to take his lunch stuff out of his school bag. First he got out his drink, then a banana, an orange, half a packet of chocolate biscuits, a Mars bar and finally his lunchbox. Monkey's lunchbox was the biggest in the school, always holding at least ten sandwiches, all of which he ate, every single day.

Johnny watched as Monkey opened his drink and began to eat the banana. Then he devoured the orange and three biscuits. Finally, without looking down, he reached for the lunchbox. As he popped open the lid, Orla's nose gave an involuntary twitch. Monkey's sense of smell, on the other hand, obviously wasn't so finely tuned.

Monkey's hand reached into the lunchbox. For a second it was as if time stood still. Snots, Enya and Johnny held their breaths. And then it happened.

Monkey's face turned white. It happened in the space of a single heartbeat, but a heartbeat that seemed to go on for ages. And then time started moving again. Monkey shot up from the steps, giving forth at the top of his lungs. From Monkey's fingers, impaled by its spines, dangled the flattened body of the hedgehog.

Orla threw up into Monkey's empty lunchbox, and Monkey threw up on top of Orla. Johnny stopped eating his lunch, his appetite suddenly gone. Enya and Snots, however, each ate another of the delicious sandwiches that had been saved from Monkey's lunchbox when they had made the swap, and winked at each other.

The teacher on yard duty came galloping across from the playground, closely followed by the entire junior-infant class. They looked at the scene, totally unimpressed, all of them under the impression that the squashed hedgehog was some kind of puppet and that Monkey was putting on a show.

Johnny and the gang decided to make themselves scarce. As they made their way out of the school, Johnny thought he could hear a sound like somebody singing in the softest voice. It was like one of those chants that they sometimes sang in church. But it was only Enya. She was singing: 'We're invincible, invincible, invincible.'

After their lunch they decided to walk through the town. Jimmy Pats Murphy had joined them, having gone home for his lunch as usual, and after they told him about the hedgehog he was disgusted that he'd missed all the excitement. As they waited at a pedestrian crossing, several police cars passed by in convoy. They counted five separate police cars, and as the last one passed they all followed it with their eyes.

'Hey, Jimmy Pats,' said Johnny, 'what do you think about all that crap that Seamus Murphy is saying about aliens landing in his garden? Monkey told us about it this morning. And what's with all the police cars?'

They were just coming to Kilfursa library, and Jimmy Pats sat down on the park bench outside its gates. They all followed suit, Johnny sitting next to Jimmy Pats, Enya sidling up to Johnny, and Snots squeezing between Enya and the metal armrest.

'Well,' said Jimmy Pats, 'as you know, Seamus Murphy is one of the most sophisticated liars in the entire world. His lies are of such a fine standard that they almost resemble the truth, and some people, my father for instance, doubt that they're lies at all. So the thing with Seamus, whether he's talking about Elvis singing at his grandfather's funeral, the spaghetti that escaped from his mother's saucepan and is living wild in the garden on a diet of mice and sparrows, or UFOs landing in Kilfursa, is that you can believe him if you choose to and disbelieve him if you don't.'

'In other words,' said Enya, 'you don't know.'

'That's not what I said,' replied Jimmy Pats, suddenly defensive.

'Yeah,' said Snots, 'but what exactly *did* you say? I mean, that sentence was so complicated that I've forgotten the question you were trying to answer in the first place.'

'What I asked him,' said Johnny, 'was, did he believe this stuff about the aliens, and what's with all the police cars? I mean, Jimmy Pats, you live up here. There's people coming into your dad's pub all the time. Surely you've heard the rumours?'

'Look,' said Jimmy Pats, 'I'll tell you the truth, and that's more than you'll get from Seamus Murphy. I haven't a clue. All I know is that for the first time in the history of the state there's more police cars than criminals. Maybe they've arrested invisible aliens and they were sitting in the back seat as the police cars passed just now. Who knows? The only thing I do know is that there's *something* going on. And as for that thing with the UFOs, all I know is that late every night and early every morning for the past week, strange lights have been seen descending north of Kilfursa, mainly around Lizard's Snout, up near where Mr McCluskey lives. And now you know as much as I do. Look, why don't you come up here for the bank holiday weekend? You can stay at my place. Maybe we could investigate this together.'

Enya had been listening with increasing interest. 'Look, you bunch of plonkers, there's no way I'm spending the long weekend up here looking at police cars and flashing lights in the sky. Give me a break!'

Johnny said nothing, but he secretly agreed with Enya. It seemed a long journey to take based on nothing but another lie from Seamus Murphy. Then he looked at his watch and announced that it was time they were heading back to school, so they all got up from the bench together and started to head back.

Class resumed without Orla and Monkey. Orla had been sent home because she couldn't wash all the little lumps of vomit out of her hair and she still smelled disgusting. Monkey had been sent to Saint Fursa's Hospital just down the road, on the orders of the school nurse, so that he could get a tetanus jab. And Mr Chamberdale had impounded the remains of the dead hedgehog, pending further investigation.

The class noticed that Mr McCluskey didn't seem too well either. His concentration kept wandering and he would spend long periods just staring out of the window. Jimmy Pats timed several of his broken sentences and discovered that the longest gap lasted just over two minutes. Jimmy Pats wrote down the beginnings and the ends of each sentence, and was surprised each time to discover that they all still made perfect sense.

Before the end of the class Mr McCluskey sat down at his desk and instructed everybody to complete the tasks in their textbooks. Jimmy Pats continued to take notes on Mr McCluskey's behaviour and noticed that he spent a lot of time scratching a particular area of his forehead.

After the afternoon break, everybody expected that Mr McCluskey would have gone home and that some

other teacher would have taken his place. Mrs Dooley, the music teacher, was the one who normally stood in for him. But everybody was wrong. Mr McCluskey had decided to muddle through till the end of the afternoon. He didn't actually teach anything, simply told everybody to read a book quietly.

Eventually the bell rang for the end of school and they all packed away their books. As he was leaving, Johnny noticed that Mr McCluskey's forehead was beaded with droplets of sweat. His eyes were bloodshot and he looked extremely unwell.

her thumbnails were five centimetres long ...

On the way home in the school bus, Johnny sat quietly in the back seat while Enya made breath-pictures on the window. Each picture bore an uncanny resemblance to Peggy Delaney and Johnny noticed that as soon as she had finished a picture, she would rub it out firmly and then start all over again. She was muttering something under her breath as she did this, but Johnny couldn't quite make out the words. He didn't know that she was intoning a spell: *I'll rub out the sun, I'll rub out the moon, and then I'll rub you out, very very soon*.

Snots was knitting a scarf. Snots was very good at knitting, having been taught by his mother, who was a dab hand at Aran jumpers. But, for some reason, he never used wool. Snots always knitted with baling twine. He had made himself a baling-twine cap and a baling-twine jumper, a baling-twine tie in the school colours and even several pairs of baling-twine gloves. The cap would nearly give you brain damage if you put it on, but Snots wore it every winter without fail. The jumper was so stiff that once he had it on he could barely move, but he stubbornly wore it on the coldest days. Snots was fiercely proud of his knitting. One year he gave Johnny a pair of baling-twine socks as a Christmas present, but they nearly cut the feet off Johnny – the only advantage he could see about knitting with baling twine was that nobody would want to steal your clothes.

Eight kilometres before Earc Luachra, Enya had fallen asleep and had begun to snore. It was a gentle kind of snoring, and her lips trembled with it. Johnny left his window and sat next to her, watching her. The spots on her face looked particularly red and angry – *no sign of a rag cure,* thought Johnny – but she seemed peaceful and untroubled. Johnny almost fell asleep

himself, listening to the *blerym-blerym* of her lips and the clicking of Snots's knitting needles. Well, he had been up half the night too.

Four kilometres from the village Enya woke up. She lifted her head and began to stretch.

'Johnny, are we at the crossroads?'

'We'll be there in about a minute. Why?'

'I want to get off and go to the church again. I want to light another candle.'

'But you haven't got your bike. You'll end up having to walk home.'

'I don't care. It's to do with the spots. It'll help the cure.' She took up her schoolbag and began to walk down the aisle of the bus. Johnny watched her go. She hadn't asked him to come with her but he knew she wanted him to.

Enya spoke to the driver, who began to slow down. Johnny got up reluctantly and took his schoolbag.

'Wait for me, Johnny,' said Snots, and he began to tidy away his knitting.

The bus pulled away at the crossroads, leaving the three of them on the grass verge. They shouldered their bags and began to walk the mile to the church. Johnny thought he saw something out of the corner of his eye, a shaft of light that wasn't there when you turned to look directly at it. He mentioned it to the others and was surprised when they said they could see it too. The light seemed to be moving with them towards the church, but disappeared after about two hundred metres.

'I wonder what that was,' said Johnny.

'Maybe it was like those things you get in your eye,' said Snots. 'You know, those little balls of grease that float about and get caught up in your vision. They're called zymotes, or something like that.'

'Yeah, I know what you mean,' said Johnny. 'But I never knew they had a name. Zymotes, that's cool!'

'Yeah,' said Enya. 'Zymotes from outer space.'

They were nearly at the church, could see its small tower just above the tops of the trees, so they quickened their pace.

There was a bicycle at the church gate. Enya immediately identified it.

'It's Peggy Delaney's. The old bag must be inside.'

'Look, Enya,' said Johnny. 'Behave yourself. Let it go.'

'But the old witch shopped us to Chamberdale. And anyway, what are you afraid of? I thought you said you were invincible.'

'Who said anything about being afraid? It's just not right to do something nasty outside a church. And most especially *inside* a church. So don't even think about it.'

'Okay, have it your way. But I'm not going to close the doors, and neither are you.'

Enya strode up the church drive and up to the door.

It was wide open. So was the one inside the porch. This changed things.

'Make sure you close the doors,' ordered Enya, 'and don't argue.'

Snots was the last one in and he closed the doors with great ceremony. Peggy Delaney was three pews up from the back. She had a black rosary beads in her clasped hands, and was praying like there was no tomorrow.

'That's a good man, Snots,' said Enya in her loudest voice. 'Wouldn't you think people would have some consideration, and close the doors when they're told. Wasn't there a load of bats inside the church only this Sunday, crapping and squeaking all over the place.'

Peggy Delaney shifted in her pew, but didn't look up. She didn't have to. She knew well enough who was there.

Enya strode up the middle of the church and began to light candles. Snots followed her, but as Snots passed Peggy Delaney, Johnny heard her say, 'Hello, there, James,' and he was surprised to hear Snots reply, 'Hi, Peggs.' Snots then went up to the front bench and knelt in a pew. Johnny wasn't the least bit surprised when Snots began to pray. He was always doing what you didn't expect him to do.

Johnny sat at the back, two seats behind Peggy Delaney. Peggy was an eccentric old widow who lived on her own and farmed a few sheep on the hilly fields around her house. A lot of people said she was a witch because she was boss-eyed and kept cats, but Johnny didn't really have anything against her – even the business about reporting him to Mr Chamberdale. The truth was, she was well within her rights, as far as he was concerned. She was just an old farming woman, that was all.

But as he looked at Peggy now, he noticed things that he hadn't really seen before. Her fingernails were short, the typical broken and blunted nails of anybody who lives on a farm and does all the work. But her thumbnails were extraordinary. They were five centimetres long and shaped into points. And he noticed something else as well. She was wearing a knitted waistcoat made entirely from baling twine.

Peggy finished her prayers and got up from her pew. She came down the church towards Johnny, moving slowly, her stout body like an enormous bell.

Johnny got up. 'Listen, Mrs Delaney, I want to say sorry about this morning.'

'You do, do you?'

'Yeah. Look, I mean it. We weren't doing anything bad. We were just getting hawthorn blossoms to clear up Enya's bad skin. I'm sorry if we woke you. Really.'

'It's not bad skin that's giving her the spots, young man. But the blossom is a good cure all the same. Anyways, that school principal of yours phoned me and told me the whole thing and I'd be inclined to

follow his judgement. For now, anyway.'

Peggy turned around and looked in Enya's direction. The candles were still stacking up.

'So, she's the one with the candles. I wondered who it was. How many does she light?'

'Thirty-three. It's her favourite number.'

'Mmmmmmm,' said Peggy, 'not a bad number at all, at all. But tell me something, and don't lie to me, is she paying for any of them candles? 'Cos the priest is complaining of coming up short.'

'Nah, she never brings any money. If I've got some, sometimes I put it in for her, but it's never enough.'

'Well,' said Peggy, 'you know what they say: The Blessed Virgin doesn't need money.' And with that she turned and made her way towards the door. However, before she got there she pointed one of her thumbnails at Johnny.

'And as for you, let me tell you this. It wasn't for climbing my wall at half-four in the morning that I reported ye to your teacher. It was for littering my land with that snotty hanky and those rags in my tree. Mark me well, don't do it again.' And then she left, making sure to close both doors with a resounding slam.

Eventually Snots had said as many prayers as he could manage and Enya had come to her thirty-third candle. Outside the church they began to make their way over the fields, a route that would cut a good kilometre off their journey.

'Listen, Snots,' said Johnny, 'I noticed that Peggy was wearing a baling-twine waistcoat. That wasn't one of yours, by any chance?'

'Of course it was, Johnny. I'm the only one, around here anyway, who knits with baling twine. She has a baling-twine skirt to match it. It wears well on the tractor.'

'Man, I didn't know you were so friendly with her.'

'Oh yeah, I've known Peggs for ages. Sure, Johnny, wasn't it Peggs who taught me how to charm insects.'

'Say that again,' said Johnny.

'How to charm insects,' said Snots. 'It's a really useful thing to be able to do. Look, I'll give you a for instance.'

They were coming to the crossing between one field and another, the division formed by an ancient, high boundary of piled stones and furze. Snots stood underneath an overhang of flowering furze and began to make a clicking sound with his mouth. In a moment the ground was swarming with beetles. They were coming from the crevices between stones, the hidey-holes beneath exposed roots, and even cutting themselves clean through the grass matting of the turf at his feet. They gathered at his shoes and began swarming up his legs. Suddenly he stopped the clicking. The beetles stopped in their path, seemed to hesitate, as if coming out of a stupor, and then began to scurry back to all the places from which they had come.

71

Johnny just stood with his mouth open. Enya, however, showed no response one way or the other, as if she had seen this kind of thing before.

'Neat trick or what?' said Snots.

It was only when they got to Earc Luachra that Johnny realised he had left his bag behind him in the church. There was nothing for it but to get his bike and cycle all the way back to retrieve it.

On the fast, downhill cycle home, Johnny noticed strange shafts of light accompanying him along the road, all the time matching his speed. He had no idea what they were, but they unsettled him. As soon as he got home he went indoors and stayed there.

That night Johnny couldn't get comfortable. He fell in and out of sleep. There was a pressure against his neck, pushing up through his pillow. Then the pillow was against his face, swallowing him. It bore him down through the blankets, through layers of sheets, twelve in all, each layer retaining the red imprint of his body, like a shadow shape. Down, down went the pillow, taking him through the floor of the house. Somewhere deep beneath the earth it vomited him up, and he floated back, through rock and soil and sheets and blankets, back up on to the tousled surface of the bed.

Johnny woke in a sweat. The pillow was cold beneath his neck and there was something lumpy beneath it that seemed to be pushing up for release.

Johnny lifted the pillow. Underneath was a doll made from strips of rags plaited together in tight, bundled knots. By the starlight from his window, Johnny looked at it in horror. He knew, without even having to pull it to pieces, that it was made from twelve strips of cloth, each strip a year of Enya's age, each strip a bloodied rag that he had tied to Peggy Delaney's tree.

Johnny opened the window, and, taking the doll by the tip of its right leg, he flung it out into the garden. It landed somewhere in the darkness.

it continued to emit its alarming squeak ...

M r McCluskey had had a bad day. Then he had had a bad night. Now he was having a bad morning. As he looked into the bathroom mirror he realised, with a spontaneous combination of disquiet and distaste, that a small screw was embedded in his forehead, about five centimetres above the outer corner of his right eye.

Feeling a little ridiculous, he placed his razor on the

edge of the sink, and, with his index finger, gingerly touched the head of the screw. It felt cold and metallic under the gentle probing of his fingertip. He realised that this could be serious. It's not every day that people find screws in their head. For a dizzy second he hesitated, looking stupidly into the mirror. He even considered, absurdly, whether or not to continue shaving.

Almost distractedly, he noticed that the bottom half of the mirror was becoming clouded, and he realised that he had left the hot tap running. He turned it off and wiped the steam from the mirror.

Oh Lord, how did this thing get here? he thought. Perhaps the screw had fallen into his head as he slept, dislodged from some fixture in the ceiling? For a brief moment he entertained this explanation, but then dismissed it as idiotic.

Well, one thing was certain. He couldn't walk around with a screw in his forehead. Mr Chamberdale would be sure to say something. Not to mention the smart remarks from his class.

With his forefinger and thumb Mr McCluskey tried turning the head of the screw, but it was in too tight and he could not move it. A second attempt merely left an impression of the screw's hard edge in the flesh of his finger. He looked about the bathroom for some instrument to help loosen the screw, and, picking up a steel nail file, he placed its flat edge, somewhat cumbersomely, into the groove in the head of the screw. Then, watching himself all the while in the mirror, he began to rotate the file.

The screw gave a nauseating squeak as it started to turn, and he instinctively pulled the nail file away and placed it on the edge of the sink. He touched the screw with a finger to confirm that it had loosened, and then he began to turn it again, with his forefinger and thumb. As the threads turned, perhaps making contact with his skull, the screw continued to emit an alarming squeak. But he persevered.

Mr McCluskey leaned closer to the mirror to get a good look at what was emerging from his skull. Curiously, there was no sign of blood clogging the threads, as he expected there would be, but the screw continued to unwind from his forehead – two centimetres, five centimetres, nine centimetres. As it reached the twelve-centimetre mark, Mr McCluskey felt something flutter inside his head, as if an enormous coil had just come unsprung.

At that moment Mr McCluskey woke up. He wasn't having a bad morning, after all. He was still having a bad night. He sat up in the darkness of his room and switched on the light.

There was a strange sensation in his head, like the after-shock of a particularly vivid nightmare.

Feeling rather stupid, he touched his forehead, but of course there was nothing there. He went to the

bathroom, ran the tap and doused his face. Although his mind was telling him that there was not, and could *never have been*, a screw in his head, he checked the mirror anyway. And just on the spot where the screw had been in his dream was a small white mole. The mole had always been there, but he was usually only vaguely aware of its existence. It was one of those things you took for granted and after a while you failed to notice it. He touched it now with his finger, but the sensation was barely perceptible.

He felt absolutely terrible, as if he was coming down with the 'flu. Suddenly he remembered being in the classroom that day and that the mole had itched like mad. That was obviously what had set off the dream. Returning to his bed he fell quickly into a sound sleep.

The following morning he didn't feel so bad. While shaving, the mirror began to steam up as the hot water spiralled into the sink. As he began to clear the steam with the sleeve of his pyjamas, he remembered the dream of the night before.

He felt a sudden panic and looked at his forehead in the mirror. There was no screw. But there was no mole either.

Johnny hoped that it would never come down ...

As soon as Johnny woke up he was mad. Mad with Enya, mad with Peggy Delaney, and just plain mad. He didn't like the idea of people putting rag dolls under his pillow. And he knew it was Peggy Delaney's doing because the doll had been made from the strips of cloth they'd tied to her tree. And this was all Enya's fault in the first place! Why the hell hadn't they just tied the stupid things to the tree he had in his *own* back garden? Or the one in Enya's? He decided to go out into the garden and get the rag doll. He'd show it to Enya and give her a real telling-off.

As soon as he was dressed he went out. There was a magpie in the hawthorn tree and it had the rag doll in its beak. When it saw Johnny it opened its wings and flew off, taking the doll with it. In a minute it was out of sight. Johnny was really mad now. He gazed up at his bedroom window. How the hell had Peggy Delaney got inside his house? He just couldn't imagine her climbing through the window. He was definitely going to have words with Enya. This whole business was getting out of hand.

At breakfast Johnny noticed something wrong with his Weetabix. He left it to get soggy in the bowl, just the way he liked it, the cereal expanding with the milk. But when he came back to the table he noticed that the bowl seemed fuller, and it looked as if someone had stirred the Weetabix around. He dipped in his spoon and brought out a green plastic dinosaur.

'Man, that's so neat,' said his brother Jerry. 'After spending sixty million years in the frozen tundra, a leaf-eating dinosaur is awoken as a result of global warming. What are the implications for mankind? Will we be able to share the earth with these enormous but gentle creatures?'

Johnny exploded. 'You little cretin. I'm sick and tired of you putting this crap in my breakfast. Can't I just have one day when I have a normal breakfast, like everyone else? If you have to play with food, play with your own food, you little moron.'

'You're the moron, Johnny Coughlan. How can I put a dinosaur in my breakfast when I'm having toast? Whoever heard of a leaf-eating dinosaur being preserved for sixty million years in a slice of toast? Get real, will you!'

'Watch it, Jerry! I'll give you a clip round the ear.'

'I'd be very careful if I was you,' Jerry said menacingly. 'I know of certain people who would be very interested to learn that certain other people were seen on the school bus with dead hedgehogs yesterday.'

'Don't threaten me, ya little twerp. I'll stick you in a jam-jar and close the lid.'

'Johnny! Jerry!' their mother's voice was sharp with exasperation. 'Stop that fighting, you two, for Heaven's sake! And finish your breakfasts. The bus is coming up the road. I can see it. Get a move on, or you'll be cycling the seventeen kilometres to school.'

'Ah Mam, will you tell him to stop! He's been putting plastic dinosaurs in my Weetabix.'

But Johnny's mother wasn't listening. 'Hurry it up, the pair of you. The bus is here.'

Jerry rushed out from the table, gathering up all the toast before Johnny could get any. Johnny followed him into the hallway, but by that time Jerry had put all four half-slices into his mouth.

'Jhustd ooo bhatdch ooor thelv,' said Jerry, through four layers of toast.

Out on the street a dense haze of noxious fumes surrounded the school bus. It was so thick that Johnny had almost to walk sideways to get through it.

As he climbed the steps of the bus something caught his eye. Through the wide windscreen, he could see that the road ahead was littered with

79

squashed hedgehogs. There were dozens of them. He made his way down to the back of the bus where Enya and Snots were sitting. *How could he get Enya away from Snots so he could talk to her about the doll?* Then he saw what was on the back seat. Arranged in a neat row between Snots and Enya were three flattened hedgehogs and a dead cat. Johnny said nothing, but sat two rows in front of them, his body turned in the seat so that he could see what they were at. Enya picked up the flattened cat and dangled it out of the window by its tail. As the bus gained speed going down a gradient, Enya let go of the cat. It spiralled out into the air, was caught by the wind like a kite, and took off into the heights of the morning sky. Johnny had never seen a flying cat before, but this one looked quite magnificent. Soon they lost sight of it, and Johnny hoped that it would never come down.

Next out the side windows went the hedgehogs. These were nowhere as graceful as the cat, but there was a kind of lethal determination in the way they skipped over the air that was equally admirable to behold.

'Well, Enya, the cat was definitely the best flyer, but the hedgehogs would be very useful as a defence mechanism if you were ever being chased by the police,' said Snots, who was entering some details into a small, hard-covered notebook. Johnny knew that he would discuss his findings later with Jimmy Pats

Murphy. The pair of them always exchanged information concerning their various experiments.

Now that the back seat was free of dead animals, Johnny thought it safe to sit down next to his friends. His chat with Enya would have to wait.

'So, what's with all the squashed animals?' asked Johnny.

'Well, if you ask me, there's something making them wander out into the open and they're just getting killed on the roads by the traffic,' said Snots. 'The mystery is, what is it that's forcing them to come out of hiding in the first place? It's like there's a pied piper around, or something.'

'What?' said Johnny, 'you mean, like the way you were charming those beetles up near Saint Fursa's church?'

This stopped Snots up for a second as he thought about it. Then he nodded. 'Yeah, Johnny, I suppose it's something like that. But the difference is, I don't harm the beetles. This thing, whatever or whoever it is, doesn't *care* about the animals. It doesn't care what happens to them. Although, to tell you the truth, I don't think it's doing it on purpose. I mean, what could it want with dead hedgehogs? It just leaves them lying around, anyway.'

'Well,' said Enya, gazing thoughtfully out through the window, 'whatever it is, it's something big. The whole road is littered with dead badgers and cats and

hedgehogs. There's a strange thing, though. I don't see any foxes. There hasn't been a single dead fox along the road.'

'Yeah, well, maybe they're just too smart,' said Johnny.

When the bus pulled up outside the school gates Jimmy Pats Murphy was already standing on the pavement instead of waiting to be collected from the pub as usual. Jimmy Pats had his notebook out and seemed keen to talk to Snots.

'My dog's gone missing,' said Jimmy Pats. *'Everybody's* dog has gone missing. There's not a dog to be found in the whole of Kilfursa, and that includes Vigrid – there's no sign of him in the school yard. And I haven't seen a single one dead on the roads, even though they're covered in every other kind of animal you could think of.'

'That kind of tallies with what me and Enya have observed,' said Snots. 'Enya noticed that there's not one dead fox on the road either. And, as you know, foxes are members of the dog family. Interesting, very interesting. Oh, by the way, on the ride over we tried out an application for squashed hedgehogs and cats. Cats are good from an artistic point of view, looking quite beautiful in flight, but hedgehogs make exemplary weapons.'

'Really?' said Jimmy Pats, leafing through his notebook. 'Well, I didn't have the benefit of a bus or aerodynamics, but I carried out several experiments with squashed rats and found that they fit perfectly inside letterboxes. I've already posted thirty-seven of them.'

Satisfied with their morning's work, they all strolled through the school gates. Johnny still had had no chance to tackle Enya about the rag-doll business.

Then, somewhere in the mayhem of pressing bodies and stray footballs, Snots was suddenly yanked by the neck and pulled to the ground. Johnny was barely aware of what was happening before a hand grabbed him too by the throat and began to throttle him. He looked up to see that the hand belonged to Monkey Murphy. While he strangled Johnny with his left hand, his right foot was planted firmly in the middle of Snots's chest, keeping him pinned to the tarmac.

Johnny noticed, in as far as he could notice anything as the life was being squeezed from him, that Monkey's right hand was covered in a cumbersome padded bandage.

'So, you two little dorks thought you could do the dirty on me, did you? Well, guess what *I* heard? I heard that this little creep under my foot was seen on the school bus with a squashed hedgehog yesterday morning. Now, isn't that a coincidence?'

The grip on his throat was so tight that Johnny couldn't speak. He could barely breathe. He thought that he would pass out at any moment. It was then

that he saw Enya coming at Monkey from behind. She leant down and took his bandaged hand. She twisted it up behind his back and squeezed as hard as she could. Monkey let go of Johnny immediately and fell to his knees in agony, Enya still holding on to his bad hand with all her strength, which was quite considerable.

Snots got up from the ground unsteadily, holding his chest. Johnny was bent over double, coughing and wheezing as he tried to get some air back in his lungs. Meanwhile, Enya just tossed Monkey roughly aside. She knew he wouldn't dare take her on. She could use her nails and teeth as well as her fists and feet. *Nobody* dared take her on.

'You complete eejit, Monkey,' said Johnny, still gasping for air. 'What dork persuaded you that we could have done that to you?'

'A little dork called Jerry Coughlan, who got a five-euro note for being so helpful.'

'My brother, Jerry? Oh, man, have you been fleeced! My little brother's an evil turd-zoid who hates my guts and will say anything to make money, of which he has quite a bit. How could we have put that thing in your lunchbox, anyway? Weren't you talking to us for most of the first break? And wasn't it me who told you about the hedgehog in the first place? As for a hedgehog on our bus, well, yeah, there could have been one. Look around you, there's dead hedgehogs *everywhere*. If you ask me, it was probably my baby brother Jerry who sold that hedgehog to Raymond Murphy in the first place.'

Enya, Johnny and Snots walked away in disgust, leaving Monkey lying in the yard, feeling very confused. He was beginning to wonder if perhaps Johnny and Snots were innocent after all. What Johnny had said made perfect sense.

Monkey got up from the ground and looked at his watch. He might have just enough time to have a word with Jerry Coughlan. Yes, just enough time.

it's from China, sir ...

Mr McCluskey watched his pupils filing into the classroom. He was not in a good mood. His forehead itched like mad and somebody had posted a dead rat through his letterbox. Regrettably, the first two periods were history, which he didn't consider ideal for inflicting agonies on bratty schoolkids. He toyed with the idea of changing the lesson to maths, but on considering the matter further and the way he

was feeling this morning, he doubted his own ability to keep up. He looked over at Johnny Coughlan, who could usually be relied on to irritate him, but Coughlan had his book opened at the appropriate page and was sitting up attentively. Enya Murphy was doing the same. As were James Murphy, aka Snots, and Jimmy Pats Murphy; they were first cousins, and eccentric loop-heads, though enthusiastic and willing pupils. Although, admittedly, one usually smelled of dead animals and the other of bleach, both had a scientific bent that Mr McCluskey admired in young minds. He scanned the classroom. In all his years of teaching he had never come across such a majority of misfits and delinquents in the one class. It was as if they were the result of an experiment that had gone horribly wrong. For all he knew, they probably were.

His gaze landed on Orla Daly, who sat at her desk with a look of such boredom that it could neutralise atomic fission. Then he spotted Monkey. Oh joy! Oh wondrous dawn! For, this morning Monkey had the look of a pupil that he could pick on without any twinge of guilt whatsoever. It was the look of the irritatingly stupid.

Monkey sat there, excavating the recesses of his ear with his left hand. His right hand, covered in the most ridiculous bandage that Mr McCluskey had ever seen, lay on the desk like a stranded dirigible.

'Ah, Michael Murphy, I see that you have returned to

us after your encounter with a prickly porcupine.'

'It was a hedgehog, sir. My hand swelled up like a balloon, sir. I coulda died, sir.'

As Mr McCluskey looked at Monkey, he felt a sudden, inexplicable surge of compassion. Something was terribly wrong. Mr McCluskey was in a bad mood and he couldn't find a single person to take it out on. It was as if some essential element had been drained from him. He realised that he would have to see a doctor as soon as possible.

At that moment a prefect came into the class with a folded note. Mr McCluskey opened the note and began to read with disinterest. Notes had lost their novelty. But then he perked up. In the note, in small, careful handwriting, Mr Chamberdale informed him that it had come to his attention that a boy – suspected of being a pupil of this school – had been seen going around the the town in the early hours of the morning posting strange objects into people's letterboxes. The note also informed him that UFOs, Unusual Flying Objects, had been observed leaving the windows of the Earc Luachra school bus. One of these objects, reliably verified by a local vet to be a dead cat, had travelled several miles through the air before landing in the bath of Mother Immaculata, Superior of the Poor Sisters of Saint Fursa. The pupils responsible in both cases had not yet been identified, but all teachers were being advised to undertake routine procedures to uncover the culprits.

All of a sudden Mr McCluskey was filled with the certainty of his true purpose in life.

'All right, class, I want everybody to empty their schoolbag on to their desk.'

Yes, there it was. Mr McCluskey felt it. A tremor pulsing through the air. Somewhere in the class somebody had skipped a heartbeat. Mr McCluskey could smell blood.

Johnny began to empty his bag. He wasn't worried, because this time, for one of the few times in his life, he didn't really have anything of an incriminating nature. However, some sixth sense was coming into play, as if he could detect the presence of thunder in the air. Out of the corner of his eye, flickering at a barely discernable frequency, was a shaft of light.

At the same time Johnny became aware of something else. Two desks ahead of him and to his left there was a movement. Jimmy Pats Murphy was leaning down and placing a flattened rat on the floor. Johnny realised that he'd have to do something quick, otherwise Jimmy Pats would be done for. Johnny put up his hand.

'Excuse me, sir, I've emptied my bag on the table, sir. But I'm busting to go to the jacks, sir. You can look through my stuff while I'm away if you want to, sir. But I definitely need to go now, sir.'

'Is that so, Coughlan. How inconvenient of your bladder, Coughlan.'

As Johnny had hoped, Mr McCluskey had

immediately become suspicious. He got up from his place and came down to Johnny's desk, standing to the right of him. Johnny could see Jimmy Pats up ahead. His back and shoulders were visibly tightening. Johnny had to get him out of this one.

'What's this, what's this?' demanded McCluskey.

'It's a comic, sir. It's Stan Kirby's *Vampire Poodle*, sir. It's considered a classic, sir.'

'A *classic*, Coughlan?' Mr McCluskey leafed through the pages in disgust, lingering momentarily on the page showing the vampire poodle biting the behind of a giant labrador.

'This is nothing but rubbish, Coughlan. *Classic* rubbish. It's like that thing you had the other day. What was it called? *Cardinal Thumb*?'

'I think you mean *Captain Finger*, sir. That's another classic, Mr McCluskey.'

'All right, Coughlan, I'm quite satisfied that there's nothing incriminating here. So empty out your pockets. Come on, Coughlan, chop-chop!'

Johnny emptied his pockets. The contents were pretty unexciting: six blackjacks, three one-cent coins, a green rubber band and a blue one, several balls of silver and gold foil from past chocolate bars, and an orange stone. McCluskey lifted the stone and looked at it coldly.

'My girlfriend gave it to me, sir.'

'I see.'

However, there was one object that Mr McCluskey found downright fascinating. It was the paper tissue that Mr Chamberdale had returned to Johnny yesterday. The paper tissue that had caused all the trouble with Peggy Delaney. Johnny had shoved it in his pocket and forgotten about it. But now it had dried out and looked like a strange chrysalis. It was as light as air and almost transparent, except for green veins that ran through its entire surface. The green veins were crystalised snots, but the whole thing had undergone such a transformation that it looked like nothing that McCluskey had ever seen.

'What's this, Coughlan? It looks almost beautiful.'

'It's from China, sir. It's called a Dream Spirit, Mr McCluskey. Enya's Aunty Felony is always sending them over. I've got loads of them. You can keep that one if you want, sir. You can put it on your desk.'

'Well, do you know something, Coughlan, I think I will. Thank you very much. This wonderful object has a ... how can I put this ... it has a kind of aura about it.'

'That's the Chinese for you, sir. Always putting auras into things.'

McCluskey held the desiccated handkerchief in his hand as if it was the greatest treasure imaginable.

'Can I go to the jacks now, sir?'

'Yes, Coughlan, off with you, boy.'

Johnny got up from his desk and began to take a few steps towards Jimmy Pats. Johnny was hoping that he wasn't the only one who'd seen the dead rat. What he needed just about now was another distraction, something to draw McCluskey's attention away for a few essential seconds. Luckily, Blister O'Flynn, sitting far to Johnny's right, had spotted the rat as well, and had guessed what was going on. Blister let his pencil-case fall to the floor. In the clatter that followed, Johnny walked forward and hooked the dead rat with his shoe. Then, praying that his aim would be true, he hefted it across the floor, where it slid to a precise stop directly underneath Monkey's chair.

Monkey didn't notice anything.

Outside, Johnny ate a few blackjacks and then congratulated himself on fobbing off an old snot-rag as a work of art. Maybe he could make a living out of it? Some artists actually did that kind of thing. He'd read about an artist who had sold her old knickers to art galleries and museums throughout the world for thousands upon thousand of dollars. Chewing on a blackjack, Johnny considered his illustrious future.

He got back to the classroom just in time to witness the fireworks. Mr McCluskey had discovered the rat and had deposited it on Monkey's desk with a ruler.

'Of course, Michael Murphy, now it's all *making sense*. And to think I was actually feeling sorry for you. There we were, thinking that you were the victim of some wicked prank, and all along you were merely the

dupe of one of your own evil experiments. So, Murphy, what were you going to do with that hedgehog before it accidentally got caught in your own fingers? Stick it down the pants of some poor innocent, no doubt.'

It was obvious from the expression on his face that Monkey had no idea what was happening to him.

'I'm sorry, sir, but I don't know what you're talking about.'

'Of course you don't, Murphy.' Mr McCluskey's voice was loaded with sarcasm. 'Does the Devil know he's a fallen angel? Now, off with you, right this second, to Mr Chamberdale, and bring this note with you. Oh, and you can take the rat as well. And don't worry, Murphy, before the day is out we'll have rounded up all the other dead rodents that you so generously donated through people's letter boxes, including the one that came through mine, and we'll return them to you.'

Snots was drawing a representation of the universe ...

During the first break Johnny went searching for Enya. She'd gone off in a hurry after class and he'd lost track of her. Eventually he found her sitting on the steps, sewing. She was sewing a small cotton doll. Through the top of its head it had one strand of human hair looped in and out of the cloth. Johnny looked down at it and exploded.

'You lunatic! What's with the dolls? What the hell is going on?'

'Calm down, will you. I'm trying to concentrate. If you don't concentrate while you're doing it then it won't work. I'm making a voodoo doll of Mr Chamberdale. It's to cure his warts. I got the idea yesterday when I found one of his hairs and his thumbprint on the page about warts in my book. He must have been sneaking a look at it when we were in his office. I've cut out the thumbprint and sewn it

inside the body and I've sewn the hair into the head. You need personal stuff like that from the subjects for the voodoo to work. Don't worry, this is *good* voodoo. Mr Chamberdale will be delighted.'

Johnny was spitting fire. 'Oh yeah, and what kind of voodoo was the doll I found under my pillow? What kind of voodoo was that?'

Enya stopped her sewing and looked up. There was a sudden look of interest on her face. 'You found a doll under your pillow? What did it look like?'

'It looked freaking scary, that's what it looked like! It nearly gave me a heart attack! I found it under my pillow in the middle of the night. It was made from those rags we tied to Peggy Delaney's tree.'

Enya put down her sewing. 'Mmmm, now that's a pity. That undoes the spell.'

Johnny was becoming exasperated. 'What spell? What are you talking about?'

'The spell to steal some of Peggy's power. She's a witch, a really powerful one. That's why we didn't use just *any* old tree. Anyway, now the spell's undone and all I've got is the soup from the blossoms.'

'Hold it a second. Are you trying to tell me that yesterday morning we were doing some kind of magic?'

'Yes, Johnny, that's what it was all about. But now Peggy's gone and reversed it. That's why she put the rags under your pillow in the shape of a doll. She put them under *your* pillow because you were my agent. You were the one who actually tied the rags to the tree. She would have known that. Anyway, it's not the end of the world. All we have to do is burn the doll in the oil from the body of three squashed toads. That'll bring the power back to our side again. So, where's the doll?'

Johnny sat down on the steps. His head was reeling and all the anger had gone from him. 'Er, what?'

'The doll, Johnny. Where's the doll?'

'I haven't got it. I threw it out the window last night and when I went to get it this morning a magpie flew off with it.'

Enya suddenly stamped both feet. 'Blast! That was Hertabese!'

'Hertabese? Who's Hertabese?' asked Johnny, beginning to lose his grasp of it all.

'Hertabese is Peggy's magpie. He's a kind of servant. It would have been Hertabese who put the doll under your pillow in the first place. Probably flew in through the window. Once Hertabese knew that you'd come into contact with the doll he knew the magic had been done. So he's taken it back to Peggy. By now she's probably soaked it in chicken fat and buried it somewhere on her land.'

'And what good does that do?'

'It seals in her magic, Johnny. Now, look, don't be worrying. You won't drop dead or anything. But I've

got to finish this doll of Mr Chamberdale. Otherwise he'll have those warts for the rest of his days. And then I need to think of some way to get back at Peggy.'

Enya began to resume her sewing and Johnny turned and left. He was still mad at her but not as much as before. And, besides, he had something else on his mind. He had to find Jerry. He had to find Jerry before Monkey did.

Johnny searched the entire school looking for his brother. No one had seen him. He eventually tracked him down. Unfortunately, Monkey had found Jerry first.

Johnny had got to the bottom of the stairs, the stairs leading to Mr Chamberdale's office, when he noticed that the floor was scattered with money. Loads of coins and the odd note. Up on the landing of the first floor he could hear Jerry's unmistakable voice. But this time it was whinging and pleading. Johnny guessed that the money was Jerry's and had somehow fallen from his pockets, so he gathered it up and put it into his own. When Johnny had collected all of the money, he sneaked as far up the stairs as he could without being seen. Sure enough, there was Jerry, hanging upside down by his feet, suspended over the stairwell in the strong left hand of Monkey. It seemed that one of Jerry's little schemes had irretrievably come undone. Johnny listened in silence. Monkey was persuading Jerry to side with him, and wasn't really giving him much of a choice. This was Monkey's first mistake. His second mistake was that Jerry was promising to do just what Monkey wanted and Monkey was lapping up every word. Monkey's third mistake was that he hadn't already collected up the money that had fallen from Jerry's pockets. To Jerry, money was everything, and promise was a funny word that he couldn't even spell and didn't even want to.

Johnny waited for the exact moment just before the bell rang for the end of break. He could hear Jerry promising Monkey faithfully that he would deliver Johnny and the gang on a plate. Although, of course, Jerry didn't actually use the word 'plate'. He used the words 'cereal bowl'. He promised to deliver 'everybody who counted', and this was an exact quote, 'inside a cereal bowl'. As Monkey let Jerry go free, Johnny slipped away. He knew that the two of them would rush straight down the stairs looking for the scattered money, and would wonder where it had disappeared to.

As Johnny made his way back to the classroom he knew two things for certain: things were still changing and he was still invincible.

The last person to enter the classroom was Monkey. He had a folded note in his hand which he handed to McCluskey. He'd obviously spent most of the break in Chamberdale's office and must have bumped into Jerry on the way down.

The note in Monkey's hand was already crumpled beyond belief. Only three people would know for certain what the note contained. Mr Chamberdale, Mr McCluskey, and of course Monkey. But whether or not any of them knew what it really meant was another question entirely.

Mr McCluskey sent Monkey to his desk and unfolded the note. He read it with an impending sense of unease. He was starting to feel the same queasiness that he had begun to feel at the same time the day before. Furthermore, he was beginning to see strange, quavering lights through the corner of his eye.

The note was very simple and at the same time dangerously complicated. It said: *Take this young man back into your class. Keep an eye on him. Keep an eye on everybody. I am beginning to see that nothing is as it seems.* And it was signed, unusually, because he never signed his notes, *Chamberdale*.

What with being let off, and having Jerry Coughlan under his control, Monkey thought that he owned the world. But that was only because he couldn't quite see where he was standing. Johnny could see very clearly where Monkey was standing. He was on the edge of a volcano, ready to slip at any moment into the fire.

When he was sure that McCluskey wasn't looking, Monkey turned around and gave Johnny the finger. Johnny took it all in his stride. He knew time was on his side.

Mr McCluskey announced that he wanted the entire class to do the exercises in their geography textbooks.

Johnny opened his textbook and started to do the exercises. On the third question he looked up to see that McCluskey was frantically scratching at a place on his forehead, up over his right eye. He also noticed that Jimmy Pats Murphy and Snots were writing in their notebooks. They had both noticed not only Mr McCluskey's erratic behaviour, but the appearance of the shafts of light moving through the edges of the classroom. Johnny could see the lights as well and noticed that there seemed to be a particularly strong concentration of them behind Mr McCluskey's desk. But, apart from himself and, undoubtedly, Snots and Jimmy Pats, no one else appeared to notice.

Johnny looked over at the girls. Enya was furtively sewing beneath her desk. She had red thread on her needle, and was sewing the shape of a heart on to the chest of the doll. Orla Daly was filing her nails.

In the hour that followed, Mr McCluskey sat in his chair, marinating in his own sweat. He hardly dared move in case it would put the room out of balance. He could feel parts of his head expand to infinite regions of outer space, and then come back into the classroom. He hoped to God that none of the pupils would notice, and felt safe in the knowledge that they had never noticed anything in the entire time he had been teaching them.

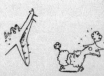

Over a period of forty-five minutes, Orla Daly filed her nails to perfection. Ants carrying grains of sand over the deserts of the Sahara could barely move as gracefully as she moved her nail file. She sat looking at her nails, thinking not a single thought.

Jimmy Pats Murphy sat converting the density of the shafts of light into mathematical dimensions. He wasn't quite sure how he was doing it, or what it all meant, but the figures just came into his head and seemed to make sense.

Snots was drawing a representation of the universe, a straight line that curved into an impossibly tight spiral. It was easy. All he had to do was move in a straight line crookedly. Inside his mind it all made sense.

Enya's sewing needle delineated a perfect heart. She glanced down at it and imagined that it pulsed.

Monkey, who, everybody knew, was a complete and utter moron, sat at his desk totally oblivious to the fact that he was a complete and utter moron. Such is the bliss of the totally stupid.

Johnny finished all of the questions in his geography book, even the last ones, which were in a little yellow box and were just for fun. The last questions were: (a) Which two figures of American popular literary culture were born in Kansas? (B) They both had dogs whose names ended in the letter O. Name the dogs. Johnny wrote down his answers: (a)

Dorothy from *The Wizard of Oz* and Superboy; (b) Toto and Krypto.

Then the bell rang for lunch, and the real world started up again.

there you are, you little maggot ...

J ohnny knew that he had a lot to do. He also knew that he could do whatever he wanted. Shafts of light played constantly in the corner of his vision and his head was filled with the strangest thoughts. Nothing was beyond his capabilities. But first he had to find Jerry. He knew that Jerry had ratted on him to Monkey, but Johnny had to somehow get Jerry back on his side.

Finding Jerry that first time had been hard. Johnny had had to search the entire school. But this time he decided to try a different tack. This time he was going to do nothing. Just wait. Because this time he knew that Jerry would be looking *for him*. Jerry had been stitched up by Monkey, and Johnny knew that his clever little moron of a brother would be searching for a way of getting his own back. He would need

allies. Johnny would be his best bet.

After a very short time Jerry stood in front of Johnny. They went and sat down by the grass verge at the edge of the school yard. The grass was cool and alive. Johnny had this weird but very definite feeling that he could hear it talking, thousands upon thousands of tiny rustling voices.

'Look, Johnny,' said Jerry, 'I've been doing a lot of thinking and I want to bury the hatchet and make up. Let's be on the same side. Let's be friends.'

'Jerry, I'm touched. Hearing you speak those words is wonderful. It really is. But, aren't you sure you'd not rather be delivering everybody *inside a cereal bowl*?'

Jerry looked at his brother with tightly slit eyes.

'You were listening,' he said.

'To every single word, you little rat.' Johnny reached into his pocket and pulled out a knotted plastic bag. 'Here's your money. Don't carry so much around with you in the future. Off with you now. And remember, no matter what, we're still brothers.'

When Johnny got up from the grass he was different. He had learned something amazing: he now knew that he both loved and hated his brother at the same time and that it would be like that forever, and that it was weird but felt kind of good at the same time.

It wasn't long before Monkey found Jerry. He was on his way to the boy's toilets.

'Ah, there you are, you little maggot.'

Jerry decided to take control. 'Listen, I'm glad we met, 'cos I've got a proposition for you. But first I want to make a few things clear. You're much bigger than me, but if you wish to work with me from now on you've got to treat me with respect. I don't like being held upside down at the top of the stairs by my ankles. That's extremely frightening when you're only nine, even when you don't let on that you're scared, but *I was*. Now, you be fair to me and I'll be fair to you, but you're never again to bully me around the place. Now, if you don't like those terms then you can pog off.'

Monkey looked at him in total disbelief. Like most bullies, he wasn't used to anyone giving him orders, and he didn't know what to do about it. Besides, Jerry had said more words than his brain could process in a lifetime.

'That sounds fair enough,' said Monkey. 'But what's this proposition you mentioned?'

This is gonna be easy, thought Jerry. 'Well, it's like this. Everybody's dog has gone missing. Including Mr Chamberdale's dog, Vigrid. Now, I'm allergic to dogs, so I can't get too close to them. But if you were to catch Vigrid then we could hold him up to ransom. Just think of the power we'd hold over Mr Chamberdale if we had his dog.'

'Yeah, but where *is* his dog?' asked Monkey.

'Finding out where the dog is, that's *my* problem,'

said Jerry. 'But once I find him you've got to catch him. That's the deal. I come up with the plan and you help me carry it out.'

Monkey scratched his head. 'Okay, I'm prepared to go with that for a while. But only as long as it doesn't take forever.'

'It won't take forever. Trust me,' said Jerry.

something profound had happened ...

M r McCluskey watched his class returning from their lunch. He had not moved from his seat since the end of the last lesson. He had eaten nothing. He simply lacked the will to move.

The class were at their desks. They waited in anticipation. With great effort, Mr McCluskey stood up. He knew that the trick was to pretend that nothing was wrong and they would never notice. He walked over to the door and turned on his heels. The entire class looked at him in awe. From the door he walked back to his desk. The class remained perfectly still.

Nobody dared move a muscle. Mr McCluskey was in control once more. He could feel the old power surging back in his body. He was dancing the dance. He was cracking the whip. He could see their faces open to the immense possibilities of learning. These were good kids. This was the reason that he had become a teacher, to see this moment – moment upon moment like this. To see the open faces of his children; to watch their minds and hearts opening up to the marvellous graces of learning. It was worth everything.

Mr McCluskey stood where he was, savouring the joy of his calling. He looked out the window. The sky was blue, and for the first time in his life he knew what that meant.

The class didn't know what to do. They had never experienced anything like this. Enya had put aside her sewing. Orla Daly watched with an overburdening interest. She thought that her brain would swell up and burst. Everyone watched. Everyone. Johnny thought it was the saddest thing he had ever seen.

Mr McCluskey had taken ten minutes to walk to the door and another ten minutes to walk back to his desk. He had moved like an old man, tired beyond imagining. For countless minutes he had stood looking out of the window. A feeble dribble of bubbled spit slid between his lips.

Johnny couldn't take another moment of this. All

the old grudges against Mr McCluskey dissolved in the face of his teacher's complete disintegration. Tears were pouring down Johnny's cheeks. He could hear his own voice, feeble as the spittle coming from Mr McCluskey's mouth. 'Sir, are you all right, sir? Do you want help, sir?'

McCluskey could hear a waterfall. It was the combined voices of all the children he had ever taught and it was beautiful.

Johnny decided that somebody should go for Mr Chamberdale. He knew that it must be him. He opended the principal's door without knocking, and when Mr Chamberdale saw Johnny at his door, his face rotting with tears, he knew that something profound had happened. He had felt this coming for days, could sense it building up. Now, he realised, he was about to look it in the eye.

'Daniel, Daniel, come with me, Daniel. Mrs Dooley will take your class. We'll get you home, Daniel.'

Mr Chamberdale looked into the vacant face of his colleague. Mr McCluskey's eyes shone, as if lit from within. The lighthouse was bursting with light, but the lighthouse-keeper was absent. And there was something else too: a noise. The classroom was filled with the crying of children. It sounded like the voices of a choir.

The class were told that Mr McCluskey had come down with a very serious dose of 'flu. A strain that came from somewhere in the Orient. His fellow teachers were told that he had had a minor mental breakdown. But it was not serious. He'd probably be back after the bank holiday weekend.

a true scientist, an investigator of the unknown ...

M rs Dooley watched over the class for the rest of the afternoon. For the first thirty minutes she kept adjusting the blinds. Most of the children in the class couldn't work out what her problem was. Except, of course, Johnny, Enya, Snots and Jimmy Pats, who knew *exactly* what she was doing. Mrs Dooley was trying to shut out the shafts of light, for she was under the impression that they were coming from outside. Snots and Jimmy Pats wrote furiously in their notebooks as she pulled down one blind, then another. Eventually she had drawn down all of the blinds until not even a squint of light could be seen through the windows. It should have been dark, but it wasn't. Mrs Dooley then decided that the columns of

light were coming through the square of glass over the door. She got a sheet of brown paper and a big blob of Blu-tack from the art cupboard, climbed on to a stool and began to block it off.

'Now, class, I want to warn you that in a second it's going to get very, very dark. I don't want to alarm you. It's just that I'm just conducting a scientific experiment.'

As the last corner of paper was stuck against the glass, Mrs Dooley looked down at the classroom of faces that were still perfectly visible to her.

Mmmmmmm, thought Mrs Dooley. Perhaps she should pursue her experiments in a different direction. She got down from the stool.

'Now, class, do we find it bright or dark?'

'Excuse me, Miss,' said Julie Hegarty, 'but what exactly *is* dark. We've kinda forgotton, Miss. It seems that these days *everything* is bright.'

Mr McCluskey would have told Julie that this was a stupid question and one he might have expected from Mr Coughlan or any of the Mr Murphys, but not from her. But Mrs Dooley didn't operate like that. *How intriguing*, she thought, *how very intriguing*.

Aloud she said, 'Now, class, I want you all to close your eyes.'

Everyone in the class closed their eyes.

'Hey, Miss,' said Monkey, whose mind seemed to be opening up to the wonderful process of thinking, 'how do we know if our eyes are closed?'

It was probably the most intelligent question Monkey would ever ask. Mrs Dooley looked at the class. Everyone, without the shadow of a doubt, had their eyes tightly closed, even Jimmy Pats Murphy, who despite this was writing rapidly into a hardcover notebook, his pen flowing unerringly from line to line. Mrs Dooley slipped off her shoes as quietly as she could and tiptoed in her bare feet across the front of the room. The whole class turned their heads to follow her progress, their eyes tightly closed.

Mrs Dooley moved to the right and the heads turned to the right. Mrs Dooley moved to the left and the heads turned to the left. This was very exciting. Oh, this was the most exciting thing that had happened to Mrs Dooley in years.

Then Mrs Dooley had a thought. She closed her eyes. Then she opened them again and closed them very quickly. She did this as fast as she could, over and over until she could hardly remember whether her eyes were open or shut. But it made no difference to what she could actually *see*. And then it dawned on her. She wasn't seeing with her eyes at all. She was seeing *with her mind*.

'Now, class,' said Mrs Dooley, 'I want you to listen very carefully because I think this is important. And I want you all to know it just in case I forget it. We do not appear to be seeing with our eyes. I think we're

seeing with our minds. To test out my theory I want us to do a little experiment while we've still got our eyes closed. I'm going to get down on my hands and knees and I want you to do the same, and when we're all down on the floor I want us all to form a train, with me in the lead. We must stay in the same order the whole time and you've got to follow me wherever I go. And you must keep *your eyes closed*.'

As far as the class were concerned, this was the best lesson they'd had in ages. For some of them it was the best lesson ever. With their eyes closed they followed Mrs Dooley all over the classroom, under desks and around desks and even over desks, and nobody fell out of sequence and nobody bumped into anybody else.

Mrs Dooley let up the blinds. Then she told the class to open their eyes. At first she expected everybody to be blinded, but when nobody was, she realised that they shouldn't have been anyway. The fact was, they had never been in the dark.

Mrs Dooley was beginning to get into her stride. She ordered everybody outside. The entire class marched down to the yard, and out in the open they attempted to repeat the manoeuvre they had just performed in the classroom. Within a few moments there was total chaos, people crashing into each other and falling all over the place.

It was quite obvious. Out in the school yard they were back to normal; when they closed their eyes they couldn't see a thing. It was only inside Mr McCluskey's classroom that they could see with their minds. Mrs Dooley spent the rest of the lesson moving the class backwards and forwards between the school yard and the classroom, trying to acclimatise them to the two conditions and getting them to recognise both. Something in her told her that this was important, but she didn't quite know why.

Half an hour before the end of the school day, Mrs Dooley sent a pupil to Mr Chamberdale's office with a note. She told the pupil not to read the note as it was private and personal, and she said that she trusted this particular pupil because she believed that person had the integrity to do as they were told.

The chosen messenger – one Jimmy Pats Murphy – not only read the note but also copied it, word for word, into his notebook. Mrs Dooley's note read: *Dear Charles, I think you should come down to Mr McCluskey's classroom right away. There's a disturbing phenomenon occurring that appears to infect anybody who enters the room. I have conducted several experiments and am quite certain of my findings. I think you may have to call in the Building Inspectors. There is also the possibility of health and safety implications. Actually, I'm quite certain of that. Indeed, it seems obvious to me that it is connected to Dan McCluskey's collapse. Please come down straight away and I will prove it to your satisfaction. Faithfully, Sheila Dooley.*

As soon as he read the note, Jimmy Pats fell in love

with Mrs Dooley. She was definitely his kind of woman. Actually, he had always fancied her, but now he was totally smitten. She was a true scientist, an investigator of the unknown. They were kindred spirits, soul-mates. He felt certain that once he had made his intentions clear to her, even her husband wouldn't stand a chance of keeping her affections.

Jimmy Pats knocked on Mr Chamberdale's door and let himself in. He presented the note and said that Mrs Dooley had sent him with a caution of the utmost urgency. Chamberdale read the note quickly and led Jimmy Pats back to the class.

When the Principal arrived, Mrs Dooley roped in the class to demonstrate her findings. They went through the entire experiment again. Chamberdale was profoundly shocked. He ordered the immediate evacuation of the classroom and called in the caretaker to seal the doors with masking tape. He closed the school ten minutes early, but told the pupils to attend school tomorrow as usual unless otherwise notified.

There was a stampede for the gates as the whole school celebrated the extra few minutes of freedom.

As Johnny made his way up the steps of the bus, Jerry caught him by the arm.

'Look, I just wanted to let you know that I'll always put you first outside the family, but I'm still gonna put crap in your cereal in the morning.'

'You got it, kid,' said Johnny, looking down at his brother. Then he noticed that Jerry had a bundle of papers in his hand, all different colours and shapes. 'Hey, Jerry, what've you got there?'

'They're posters. I've been pulling them off the lamposts. They're all over the place. People looking for their lost dogs. They're offering rewards. I'm thinking of maybe looking for them.'

'But, Jerry, you're scared bloodless of dogs. You're even scared of chihuahuas.'

'I know. But I'm working on a plan. That moron Monkey gets on with dogs like he was one himself. Maybe I could use him to help me. Actually, that's what I'm aiming at.'

'Bad plan,' said Johnny. 'Think of another one. Monkey's too dangerous. Don't go there.' By now they were near their seats so Johnny went to the back and sat down.

i've been having all these kinds of delusions ...

As the school bus pulled out on the main road, a convoy of three police cars gave way. Johnny looked at them through the rear window of the bus and he noticed something curious. The police cars seemed to be phasing in and out. It was like watching the television and then suddenly losing the picture. As an experiment he asked Snots and Enya to look out the back window to see if they'd notice it. They didn't seem to know what Johnny was talking about, but he persevered.

'Keep looking at them; they don't seem real or something.'

Enya was about to say something smart but then she had a thought. Maybe this was a bit like witchcraft or voodoo. So she kept looking, but the police cars stayed constantly behind the bus. Snots however, got the hang of it.

'Hey, Enya, he's right. They're phasing in and out. What you've got to do is fix your gaze on one spot and kind of go boss-eyed. It's just like looking at those Magic Eye pictures that you get in the newspapers.'

Enya tried this and after a while she had the hang of it too. The police cars were blipping in and out. One moment they were there, the next they weren't. And once their minds were alerted to this they didn't have to strain their eyes anymore. They could just see it as plain as day.

'Hey, Snots, what do you think it means?' asked Johnny.

'There's only one thing it can mean. They're not real. I'd say they're some kind of very clever broadcast. Some type of hologram. Hey, call your little brother down. Let's find out what he sees.'

Jerry came down as requested and looked out the back window. Johnny insisted that he keep looking for a few minutes.

'It's three police cars. Big deal! What do you think I am, a kid?' Jerry turned around in disgust and went back to his seat.

'I don't get it,' said Johnny. 'He's not seeing *what we see*. He thinks they're real.'

'Yeah, Johnny,' said Snots. 'But we only saw that they weren't real after doing all that stuff with Mrs Dooley. I think it must have broken some kind of

conditioning. There's definitely a lot of weird stuff going on. And if you ask me, I think Mr McCluskey is in some kind of trouble.'

'Yeah,' said Enya. 'Oriental 'flu, my eye!'

The police cars pulled off at the next crossroads, and Johnny watched them go, flicking in and out of existence like a dodgy bedside lamp.

Snots was intrigued. 'They must be programmed to drive all over Kilfursa. It's amazing, if you think about it. They're nothing but holographic images, but no one's going to drive through one because every driver on the road thinks they're real and just keeps their distance like you would *with a real car*.'

Enya was looking out the side window, her features thoughtful.

'Look,' she said finally, 'this really is more serious than maybe we've been facing up to. Just think about a few things. For instance, everybody thinks there's dozens of extra police cars driving about the roads late into the night, but how come the police haven't investigated it themselves? I mean, they'd know that they weren't real, 'cos they know how may cars they've got and how many are on patrol at any one time.'

'What are you saying, Enya? I don't get what you're driving at,' said Johnny.

'Well, I don't really know myself, but I'm wondering if maybe the police are being conditioned as well. And another thing, there must be a *point* to all these phantom cars. They must have a purpose. And they don't seem to be anywhere else but up here in Kilfursa. But they can't be actually *doing* anything, because they're not real. They can't be, like, protecting something. So maybe they're just a *decoy* to put people off the scent of the real thing that's happening.

'And if they're just an illusion, then maybe all those lights falling out of the sky in Kilfursa are the same thing. I mean, everybody's looking at Kilfursa. But what if there's nothing much happening up in Kilfursa, or not as much as we thought? What if all the real stuff is happening somewhere else? Down in Earc Luachra, for example? Look, when we get to the crossroads I think we should get off and check out the road to the church. That's where we saw those same shafts of light that we get in the school.'

The others were listening, trying to work out what she was getting at. But Enya wasn't finished yet.

'I didn't like what happened to McCluskey today,' she continued, 'even if he is an old bore who drives us mental with homework. I think something's being done to us all and I don't like it. I don't want anyone messing with my head. I feel sick and really funny and my spots are just getting worse and worse. I think it's time we fought back. Us and Jimmy Pats. He's smart.'

'I'm with you on that one,' said Johnny. 'But first we've got to find out what we're fighting. And we'll

have to find some way to protect ourselves. I've been going around as if I was invincible, but it's not true, is it? We're not invincible, are we? We're just a bunch of school kids.'

Johnny suddenly felt insignificant and scared. The thing was, nothing *had* changed. He was still a useless twelve-year-old school kid. That wish had just been a lie. A great big lie that had made a fool out of him.

'You're right, Johnny,' said Snots, sounding totally depressed. 'What can we do?'

Enya looked at them both in astonishment. She hated to see Johnny like this, and, anyway, quitting just wasn't in her vocabulary. She was a warrior.

'Get a grip, you plonkers. We *are* invincible. Say it and you believe it. We're bloody well invincible. And I know what you're thinking, Johnny; you're thinking that that shooting star was a cod. Yeah, well it was. But *your wish* wasn't. Your wish was what you wanted. Well, I want it too. So, what are we then?'

'We're bloody invincible,' said Johnny, and he gave her a friendly dig in the arm.

Snots rubbed his nose with his sleeve, bursting a ballooning green bubble. 'Yeah, okay, we're invincible. We're going to get off at the crossroads and walk down to the church right through the middle of those creepy shafts of light and I'm not going to be scared. And if I am scared, if I'm crappin' my pants with fear, then I'm still going to do it. 'Cos those shafts of light can charm hedgehogs to their deaths, but I can charm things myself. You saw me do it yesterday. I'm cool, I am. And yeah, we'll put our minds to it and we'll beat those lights.'

does anyone want a jelly shoe? ...

Jerry came down to the back seat. He stood in front of the three of them.

'Hey,' he stated, 'there's something going on. That time you called me down and showed me the police cars. Well, I could see what was happening to them, but I didn't let on. I've been seeing them since *yesterday*. They're just like those Magic Eye pictures you get in the Sunday magazines. I worked it out all by myself 'cos I'm smart. But I don't want to be smart on my own. There's no one up there in the middle of the bus that's as smart as me. None of them know what's going on. They're a bunch of losers. I want to stay down here with you. I want to join the gang.'

Johnny looked up at his little brother. Jerry was as smart as Jimmy Pats and Snots put together, and he was as fearless and cunning as Enya. With him around, the shafts of light wouldn't stand a chance.

'Okay, brother, you're on the team.'

Jerry sat down on the back seat. He could see the whole of the bus from here. He could see all of the other kids, the kids he usually sat with. Seeing the backs of their heads felt good. He could get used to sitting in this seat. There was loads of room and he was with the big kids. And not morons like Monkey. But *smart* big kids. He felt like a rock star.

'Oh yeah, one other thing,' said Jerry. 'These aliens. Does anyone have any idea what they use for money?'

Jerry could be a real smart-arse, but he was pathologically incapable of being *out*smarted. Johnny was glad that they were friends, although he knew that it wouldn't last forever, because Jerry was too much of an opportunist. But he was glad to have his brother working on his side for now. He was glad about something else too. He was glad that he had given Jerry back his money. He felt like a big brother again. Sometimes it was good being a big brother. Everyone always talked about how bad little brothers always had it, but it was hard being a big brother too. Being a big brother wasn't a condition; it was more of a job, because you had responsibilities. And today he'd felt that he'd done a pretty good job at being a big brother.

'Does anyone want a jelly shoe?' asked Jerry, pulling a crumpled paper bag from his pocket. He might as well start early if he was going to get control of this gang. Everyone dipped into the bag and took a sweet, except for Enya, who took five. There was a jelly shoe caught between each finger, and a further two squashed up against her palm by her thumb.

Jerry looked at her with admiration.

'Good technique,' he said.

it's like putting good luck into the bank ...

Snots got out his knitting. Jerry watched him for a minute or two before enquiring what he was at.

'It's a scarf,' said Snots, wondering why this wasn't obvious.

'Yeah, right,' said Jerry. 'So, who's it for, then? You knitting it for a scarecrow or something?'

'Nah, it's for me,' said Snots, suddenly realising what Jerry's problem was. 'I knit all my stuff in baling twine. It's much more durable than wool.'

'How long would it take to make a pair of trousers?' said Jerry, and then quickly added, 'in *my size*.'

Johnny turned his head, suddenly interested. He knew that Jerry was scheming.

'Well,' said Snots, 'I would term that question a consultation, and a consultation will cost you two jelly shoes.'

Jerry took the bag from his pocket and handed Snots a jelly shoe.

'I'll give you one jelly shoe now, and the second one when the consultation is over,' said Jerry, without putting the bag back in his pocket.

'Okay,' said Snots, taking the jelly shoe. 'Let's see. If I was knitting for myself I'd take days and days 'cos it's for myself and there's no hurry. But if I was commissioned to do trousers in your size I'd have it ready by tomorrow. You'd get it by the time we'd reached the church crossroads on the way home from school. It would cost five euro, and I would supply the baling twine. But you'd have to give me the rest of your jelly shoes as a sign of good faith. And, by the way, if you wanted a zip you'd have to pay an extra two euro, but personally I would consider a zip a wasteful extravagance. I normally knit trousers with a kind of bootlace thing at the front and that ties them as well as anything. Now, that's the end of the consultation, so could I please have my second jelly shoe, as agreed?'

Jerry took a jelly shoe out of the bag and gave it to Snots. Snots put the two jelly shoes he now had into his mouth.

'Vanks,' said Snots.

Then Jerry handed the entire bag over to Snots and said, 'Consider yourself commissioned. And if you make them with elasticated bottoms on the legs, I'll give you an extra euro.'

Johnny looked at Jerry in absolute amazement. 'What the hell do you want a pair of baling-twine trousers for?'

But Jerry said nothing, only sat back in his seat, his eyes taking on the distant glaze of someone who one day plans to rule the world.

Snots emptied the bag of jelly shoes on to the seat next to him. Out they came with a loose cascade of sugar. There were sixteen jelly shoes left, and he divided them equally between everyone, making four for each, including Jerry. Johnny and Enya took theirs with thanks but with no further comment. They weren't the least bit surprised because Snots was always doing this kind of thing. Jerry, however, was completely wrong-footed.

'What's this for?'

'It's for karma,' said Snots, licking the end of his finger and dipping it into the loose sugar scattered across the seat.

'What's karma?'

Snots brought his sugary finger up to his mouth and sucked it thoughtfully before answering.

'Well, it's like good luck. It's like putting good luck

into the bank. You put karma into the bank and it gains interest. Then you live off the interest of your good luck.'

Jerry considered this very carefully. This was a new angle for him, but he understood it perfectly. He'd never considered luck to be like money, but now that Snots had put it that way it made perfect sense. And the idea of *making luck*, of collecting loads and loads of it till you were rich *with luck*, was something he could work with.

'Here,' said Jerry, giving one of the jelly shoes back to Snots. 'This is for karma.'

Snots put the jelly shoe straight into his mouth and got back to his knitting. Jerry, realising that the conversation was over, got a book out of his schoolbag and began to read. The title on the cover was *One Hundred Ways To Make Money During Your School Holidays*.

Johnny sat back in his seat, taking it all in, eyeing Jerry up and down and not quite knowing if this new situation was going to be a good thing or a bad thing. Meanwhile, Snots was undertaking the first stages that would transform his scarf into a trouser leg.

Enya had dozed off, her head resting against the window. Johnny got up and sat next to her, his arms folded, his head leaning against the back window.

About five minutes before the church cross, the bus began to slow down, before pulling into a layby. The driver got out to stretch his legs and sat on a large rock by the side of the road, smoking a cigarette. Five cigarettes later, he was still there. He looked stressed, his face pale.

Jerry went across to him. 'Have we broken down or something?'

'No, son, it's okay, just get back on the bus. I'll be with you in a minute. I'm just taking a breather,' said the driver.

'Have you got a headache?' asked Jerry, thinking that this sudden concern might gain him some karma.

'Nah, nothing like that. I've just got a bit of eye-strain, that's all. It must be the sun. I've been catching lights in the corner of my eyes all the way from Kilfursa.'

Jerry turned and got back on the bus, making his way down to the others. 'The driver's seen the lights. They've been following him along the road all the way from the school. He thinks it's the sun or something. They've bedazzled the bejaybers out of him.'

Snots looked worried. 'So, it's spreading,' he said.

The driver came on board again and the bus set off. Everyone on the back seat was looking at the road through the corner of their eyes. Two enormous, snaking shafts of light were following on either side of the road, like two lengths of invisible ribbon, all the way from Kilfursa.

At the church cross the four of them got off the bus.

125

Snots was last because he'd had to pack away his knitting. He was very excited about making the trousers for Jerry. The outfit he'd made for Peggy Delaney had been a present. He'd never had an actual commission before. Maybe Jerry would spark some kind of demand, and everybody would be looking for baling-twine clothing. He had no idea what Jerry needed the trousers for, but hoped it was for something he'd be doing in public, so everyone would get to see them. He wondered if he should design a label, and sew it to the inside of his clothing. He'd never considered it before, but perhaps now was the appropriate time. Maybe something like: *Divine Twine by James Murphy*.

'Snots, are you coming, or what?' called Johnny. 'Hurry up, we're smothering in exhaust fumes!'

Snots stepped off the bus into the blue, choking cloud.

The bus pulled away, and the cloud of exhaust dissipated, drawn by the wind. As the smoke filtered through them, the shafts of light stood out more clearly.

'It's a pity there isn't fog,' said Snots. 'That way we'd see the lights, *no problem*.'

'It doesn't matter if we can see them or not,' said Enya, sounding extremely narked. 'The fact is, we *know* that they're there. We'll find some way of dealing with them. Look, let's just go to the church.'

Johnny thought of the rag doll and shivered ...

A little way down the lane they came across a badger. Its body had been crushed by cars repeatedly driving over it, and its spilled insides had been eaten by crows, two of which were now on the road, scraping the tarmac with their beaks. The crows left it till the last minute before taking off. They left the ground slowly, gathering up the air with ease, turning their heads from side to side and summing up the four intruders before taking the short flight to a nearby tree. From the tree they looked back down on to the road.

Snots, who was very comfortable with animals, whether they were alive or dead, began to peel the badger's pelt from the road. It came off in one piece.

'Wotcha' doing that for?' asked Jerry.

'I'm taking it down to the church,' said Snots. 'It's not right to leave it here on the road with those stupid

127

crows and the cars just driving over and over it. I'm taking it to the graveyard.'

Jerry became suddenly enthusiastic. 'Here, I'll help you carry it. We'll be like them whatyamacallits you get at funerals.'

'Pall-bearers,' said Johnny.

So Snots and Jerry walked either side of the flattened badger, bearing him down to the church. Johnny and Enya followed behind, edging close together. They looked like the chief mourners.

The two crows waited for them to pass and then returned to the road, teasing the last of the squashed meat into their beaks.

As the small funeral procession came to the gates of the church, Johnny noticed something lying in the grass. It was Peggy Delaney's bicycle. A linnet flew down from somewhere beyond the gable of the church and landed on the handlebars. The church gates were open, so they passed through.

They marched down to the small graveyard which was reserved for members of the clergy, mainly the priests who had served the parish by ministering from this church. They came to the space between the graves of Archdeacon Maurice Murphy and Father Enda Murphy.

The Archdeacon's headstone was quite large, an imposing Celtic cross which had been purchased by his family. On it was inscribed: *Archdeacon Maurice*

Bartholomew Murphy, 1869-1930. Author of Jesus Amongst Snakes *and* The Quare Curate. *Died on the 7th February, after slipping from the presbytery roof while trying to rescue a near-frozen magpie.*

Father Enda Murphy merely had a small stone which read: *Father Enda Murphy. 1910-1958. Parish priest from 1949-1958, who died after crashing his motorbike. With the Grace of God he is now in Heaven with the spirit of his severed arm.*

It always amazed Johnny to think that Father Enda was driving his motorbike for six years with only one arm. When Johnny had asked his father how he had managed it, his father had sighed in admiration and said, 'Ah, that Father Enda could balance on a pin. If there's a circus in Heaven he's probably on the high-wire.'

Enya went off to the side of the church and found a shovel. Its handle was bleached white from exposure to the elements and its blade was eaten with rust from being left out in the rain. Enya began to dig a small, new grave between Father Enda's and the Archdeacon's.

'I can do that if you want,' said Johnny.

'Nah, I'll be much quicker.'

First she cut out the turves of grass and left them to the side in a neat pile. Then she excavated an oblong hole just slightly larger than the squashed badger. She went down about twenty centimetres. Whenever she

came to a largish stone, she would tease it on to the shovel and peg it over her shoulder into the hedges on the far side of the gravestones. Her workmanship at digging was quite wonderful. If she'd left Johnny at it, he would have produced a messy, uneven hole.

When she had finished she stood to one side and Snots arranged the body of the badger at the bottom of the grave. Jerry stood by with a few wildflowers, mainly piss-a-beds and buttercups, which Snots had instructed him to pick, and they all took a few from the bunch. They stood around in a circle and dropped their flowers over the body. Then Enya took up the shovel and began to fill in the hole. When she had finished she replaced the turves of grass, as neatly as she could, and stood back.

It was then that Johnny saw Peggy Delaney. She was standing to the side watching the whole proceedings, her hands clasped in prayer, her rosary beads swinging gently from her fingers. She looked like a harmless, dotty old lady, except for those talon-like tumbnails. Johnny thought of the rag doll and shivered.

'As Jerry is the youngest, I think he should say a few prayers,' said Snots.

Jerry came forward. He placed the palms of his hands together, facing heaven-wards. He looked angelic, but Johnny knew that it was merely an illusion.

'Let us pray,' said Jerry, piously. 'I hope you rest in

peace. I hope that God is a badger. I hope you go to Heaven. Amen.'

Everybody else joined in the Amen, including Peggy Delaney. Jerry was trying to calculate by how much this would increase his karma bank account. He hoped that it was lots.

'A badger, was it, James?'

'Yes, Peggs,' said Snots. 'It died in a traffic accident.'

'Ah, the poor cratur,' said Peggy. 'I'd often be talking to them, and do ye know, they haven't a clue about this traffic business. They think that cars are great big beetles, so they do. I'm always telling them to keep clear of the roads and usually they're quite good.'

'I think something's goading them,' said Snots.

'Do ye, now?' Peggy's boss-eyes moved closer together as she looked hard at Snots. 'Well, you're right on that one, me lad,' she said. Johnny regarded her warily. She caught his eye and held his gaze steadily, her face serious. Then, unexpectedly, she gave him a wink. She turned abruptly and went to her bike. Soon she was heading out through the gates and down the road. On her bicycle she moved like the wind. Not a single person in the whole of Kilfursa could pass her out on a bike.

'Did she just say she talks to badgers?' said Jerry.

'Yeah, so what?' said Enya.

They all turned round and went into the church, Jerry coming up last. He was beginning to see that

hanging around with the older kids was far more interesting than he had imagined. It was such a relief to be with smart people for a change.

Inside the church Snots had already lit a candle for the badger, and was now kneeling in front of the altar saying his prayers. He hadn't had any money for the candle, so he'd left two jelly shoes on top of the box instead. These were duly eaten by Enya as she started lighting her own candles.

By the time Jerry came in, things were already in progress and he sat at the back with Johnny.

'What's with the candles?' he asked.

'Enya's lighting them for a personal intention. She always lights thirty-three,' answered Johnny.

'Wow. It must be a big intention. How much is that gonna cost her?'

'She doesn't have any money. She's relying on Our Lady to turn a blind eye.'

'Mmmmm,' said Jerry.

Jerry got up from his seat and unhitched his schoolbag from off his back. He found his bag of money and began counting out coins. He set a specific amount to one side, packed away the rest and took the coins up to the front of the church where he began to deposit them, one by one, into the candle box.

'What's that for?' asked Enya.

'Karma,' said Jerry.

When Jerry came back down, Johnny said, 'Listen

Jerry, if you don't go easy on that karma you'll go broke.'

But Jerry wasn't listening. He loved this karma business; it gave him a kind of buzz. It was even better than gambling.

Soon they had left the church, the gates and the doors wide open, and were making their way through the fields.

'Okay lads, this is the plan,' said Johnny. 'Snots can phone Jimmy Pats and tell him what we know, and we can work out what we're gonna do tomorrow when we get to Kilfursa. But come round to our house after your supper and we'll decide if we can do anything tonight in Earc Luachra.'

she had to go back into the kitchen ...

When Johnny and Jerry got home, their mother eyed them with suspicion. She had seen them coming up the drive, chatting away in what appeared to be a friendly fashion, There was no squabbling,

none of the usual duel-to-the-death to be the first to ring the doorbell. Something was wrong. Now, an observer might expect Mrs Coughlan to be happy to see her two boys finally getting along. But she wasn't. She wasn't the least bit thankful, because, the way she looked at it, as long as they were at each other's throats at least one of them would be allied to her. That way, at least she'd know what was going on.

She gave them their dinner and sat in the corner trying her best to overhear anything they said. But they said nothing. They just ate. Which, for Jerry, was completely unheard of. Not once did he put any inedible objects into either his own dinner or his brother's, but just sat there eating like a normal person. It was such a surprise that their mother could only manage to watch it for a few minutes at a time, and had to leave the kitchen with a cup of tea in order to recover her composure.

After supper they went into the living room together. Jerry watched the telly, while Johnny started to read that week's edition of their local newspaper, *The Ballynought Review*. Most of the stuff in it wasn't worth reading; he only looked at it for the sport results and to see what was on at the cinema in Kilfursa. But tonight he was stopped in his tracks by a headline at the top of page five: MYSTERY IN THE SKY DEEPENS WITH EERIE NIGHT-TIME SIGHTINGS IN KILFURSA.

'Hey, Jerry, come over here and take a look at this.'

Jerry left his chair and sat on the sofa next to Johnny, reading the newspaper. At that moment their mother came in and saw them reading the paper together. She was so flabbergasted that she had to go back into the kitchen and make another cup of tea.

The article went as follows:

Mysterious occurrences have been escalating over the past week in the area of Kilfursa Town, most especially in Lizard's Snout and in both Lizard's Ear East and Lizard's Ear West.

Strange lights have been reported falling from the skies late at night and in the early hours of the morning. Seamus Murphy Snr and his son, thirteen-year-old Seamus Murphy Jnr, of Lizard's Ear East, both witnessed one of these lights landing in their back garden.

'It looked like it was composed of molten glass,' said Seamus Murphy Snr. 'It was oscillating at tremendous speed and began to pass into the ground. By the time we had run out into the garden it had disappeared completely into the earth. I checked the whole place over and over again with a flashlight, but could find no evidence of where it had been. It was quite extraordinary, there was not even one blade of grass turned down by its passing. My son Seamus was with me all the time.'

Seamus took up the story from there: 'My dad was pacing up and down with the torch but we couldn't find a thing. Then I thought to myself, maybe I can hear it if it's still under the ground and making a noise. So I put my ear to

the ground and I noticed straight away that the ground was warm against my ear. Then all my hair stood on end like it does if you get static electricity, and beneath the ground I could hear a loud humming sound, like something you'd get from a beehive. I told Dad and then he put his ear to the ground and he heard it too.'

This is not the first time that strange occurrences have been reported in the Murphys' back garden. As regular readers of The Ballynought Review will know, last year Seamus Murphy Snr claimed that a saucepan of spaghetti had escaped off the hob in the kitchen and was living wild amongst the hydrangeas. Many neighbours had claimed that it was terrorising their pets, but it was never apprehended.

Meanwhile, the Kilfursa Garda have strenuously denied reports of extra police night-time activity on the streets of Kilfursa. When questioned about this alleged Garda involvement by The Ballynought Review, Chief Inspector Sean Murphy-Sullivan said: 'There are absolutely no extra Garda cars on the roads at this time, and such reports are absurd and groundless. As to the reports of strange lights over Kilfursa, we have not once been contacted by a member of the public on this matter, but we would investigate immediately if we felt such action was warranted.'

However, some residents of Kilfursa and the greater Ballynought area had another theory as to what was behind the whole thing. Dennis Murphy, proprietor of Kilfursa Educational Book Supplies was quite candid:

'Well, if you ask me, I reckon it's all just a stunt by Shaughnessy-Shaughnessy O'Shaughnessy to drum up business for his next science-fiction novel. Everybody knows that he's living somewhere in the Ballynought district.'

The Ballynought Review *contacted Mr O'Shaughnessy's publishers, The Raven's Beak Press in Dublin, but they declined to comment. Mr O'Shaughnessy's last novel,* The Snot Vampires, *is currently being made into a big-budget movie starring Val Kilmer.*

Johnny was intrigued by the reference to Shaughnessy-Shaughnessy O'Shaughnessy, who was his all-time favourite writer. He'd read all his books and short stories and even named his band, The Dead Crocodiles, after an O'Shaughnessy novel. There had been rumours for years that he was living in the area, but nobody knew where. He was as elusive as those shafts of light.

'Here,' said Jerry, 'what do you think about that Shaughnessy-Shaughnessy O'Shaughnessy stuff?'

'It's just a load of rubbish. Adults can never believe in things like UFOs and ghosts, and they're always passing them off as publicity stunts or gimmicks. It's their easy way out. It saves them the bother of having to investigate these things. Anyway, we've seen the shafts of light and the police cars that flick on and off. There's no way that Shaughnessy-Shaughnessy O'Shaughnessy is behind all that. But it's a real pity we can't tell him what we know. I bet *he'd* think of a way to fix it all.'

'Yeah, and those two plonkers, Seamus Murphy and that stupid dad of his. They're making the whole thing look like a joke.'

'You always get liars like the Seamus Murphys who try to cash in on anything that's happening. And you're right; no one's going to take this thing seriously after reading what those two pallookas said. Man, the eejits! But, the funny thing is, they might even be telling the truth this time, but no one's gonna believe it.'

At that moment their mother came into the living room again, but this time she had a cup of tea already with her. Which was just as well, because she had only that minute heard her two sons soberly discussing something they had read together in the local paper, and her head was reeling.

The telephone rang. Mrs Coughlan went to the hall to answer it. 'Johnny, it's your friend, Jimmy Pats,' she called.

Johnny came out and took the phone. Jerry followed him and sat on the stairs listening, with not a word of complaint from Johnny. Their mother went into the kitchen and put the kettle on.

'Hi, Jimmy. Yeah, so you heard from Snots. Well, what do you think?'

'Well, Johnny, I began to notice the flickering Garda cars myself, but no one else in our class who I've talked to up here seems to know what I'm on about, except Snots and now you. I think maybe there's only a few of us who are snapping out of whatever trance we were in. Snots told me that you were discussing having me come down and hang out with you in Earc Luachra. Maybe I can come down tomorrow evening when we break up for the weekend? We can talk about it tomorrow. I'll have a word with my parents tonight. Tell Snots to do the same, and I can stay at his place. And tomorrow we can do some research in Kilfursa library about UFOs and stuff like that. Or maybe even the museum. Anyway, did you see that crap in *The Ballynought Review*?'

'Yeah, I did. Oh, and Jimmy, I don't know if Snots told you or not, but my brother Jerry is definitely on our side. We'll be working together.'

'Well, that's good. But you better warn him: Monkey's put the word out up here that he's in partnership with Jerry over a surefire way to get some cash. So tell him to tread carefully. Monkey's a headcase and he'll get really narked if he finds he's being made a fool of.'

'Yeah, okay. Listen, Jerry's right beside me at the phone, so he's heard it all. We'll be careful. I'm getting together with the lads later so we'll see if we can come up with any more plans. I'll tell you in the morning. Bye.'

Johnny hung up and they both went back to the living room to watch the telly. After a few minutes the doorbell rang. Mrs Coughlan opened the door to find

Snots standing there, looking extremely flustered. She let him in and sent him straight through to the living room.

'Hey, Snots, what's up?' asked Johnny.

'Well, Enya's been trying to ring you but your phone was engaged, so she sent me to come and get you. She's in a complete panic. Her pet crocodile, Gristle Bonehead, has gone missing. When she went to his cage after getting home she found that it was full of dents and broken bits of wire and the door was smashed open. It looks like he was in a fury to get away. She's totally frantic trying to find him. I told her I'd get you and we'd go to her place. She's in the fields below her house, searching for Gristle.

Snots had brought his bike, so the two brothers got theirs and they made their way to Enya's.

'i don't like this,' said Johnny ...

When they got there they found Enya in the lower fields, in a total tizzy.

'There's no sign of him anywhere, Johnny. We've got to get to him before he eats somebody.'

Jerry was a little concerned. 'Hey, what if he eats *us*?'

'He won't touch you as long as you're with me. I just can't figure why he wanted to get out. He's made a total mess of his cage. And it's not like he's cooped up. I mean, his cage takes up the whole garden.'

'Well, Enya,' said Snots, 'if you ask me, he's probably being led by the same thing that's driving all the animals nuts around here.'

'Ah, Johnny,' said Enya, nearly in tears, 'he could get run over by a truck or something! We've got to find him.'

Johnny had never seen her cry before, didn't even think it was something she could do.

'Look, Enya, calm down. We'll help you. We're

working as a team, remember. Now, the first thing we've got to do is think this through properly. We can't just go running all over the place. I mean, Gristle could be anywhere. What we've got to do is try and figure out where's the most likely place he would go to. Snots, have you any ideas?'

'Well, because he's a crocodile he'll probably be quite safe from cars and stuff,' said Snots, "cos he'll have no business going on the road. My guess is that he'll head straight for water. And there are two bodies of water around here. There's Tip Lake just north of the village and there's the Pits, just above our houses. There's no way we could search Tip Lake this evening; it's too big, and, anyway, if he's in there he's quite safe. He'll have plenty to eat with all the fish, and even a six-foot pike wouldn't pick on a crocodile. I reckon we should check out the Pits 'cos they're nearer and we can eliminate them quite quickly. What do *you* think, Enya?'

Enya wasn't so tearful anymore. She'd got her old attitude back and was standing up straight-backed and ready to kill anything that got in her way. 'Let's try the Pits.'

The Pits were three disused quarries, their wide basins filled with water. They were situated in the high ground just above the Saint Fursa Estate, where both Snots and Enya lived. The climb up wasn't too taxing, but the four friends found themselves dragging their heels.

'I feel really funny,' said Jerry, 'and before you say anything, it isn't because I'm scared.'

'Yeah,' said Enya, 'I feel it too. I feel like there's something holding me back.'

Snots and Johnny felt the same.

'It's really weird,' said Johnny. 'It's as if there's an invisible barrier or something. But, whatever it is, I reckon we should just try to push past it and get to the top of the Pits. If there's any danger, well, we can turn around and run like the clappers. It's all downhill from here. Anyway, once we get above the Pits we'll be able to more or less see everything without going down into them.'

Everyone pushed on. Enya took the lead, the others lagging behind, with Jerry last of all. Enya reached the top first and waited for the others. When they came close to her they could see that her jaw was set. Something was amiss.

'Lads, you'd better take a look at this.'

Down in the Pits the water lay still and dark, perfect for frogs and biting insects. Thick water-grasses clogged the fringes, the water disturbed only by the odd trickle of grit that the four of them sent down from their places at the top.

Resting above the surface of the water were thousands of shafts of light, thin wafers floating on their edges, stacked one against the other, like dominoes. Their lights were so concentrated that they

could be seen quite clearly, straight on. But as bright as they were, they cast no reflection; the water directly beneath them was as dark as on the darkest night.

'I don't like this,' said Johnny. 'This is scary. I think we should get out of here.'

'Wow,' said Snots. 'This must be where all those lights that we've been seeing came from. But this feels different, kind of threatening. I agree with Johnny. Let's get out of here. And don't worry about Gristle, Enya. I reckon if he was down there we'd see him quite clearly from up here. Crocodiles cruise on the surface of the water, and their snouts are visible. And you can see there's nothing down there. Anyway, now that I'm looking at them, the banks are too steep. This isn't a suitable place for him. I figure our best bet is Tip Lake. Let's get going.'

'Not so fast,' said Enya. 'If we leave 'cos we're scared, we'll never be able to do *anything*. Let's look at them for a minute or two, and then we'll leave at our ease. I can feel them trying to spook us, trying to send us away. I think they're as scared of us as much as we're scared of them.'

'I hope so,' said Jerry.

Johnny looked over at him and saw that Jerry was shaking; he was really scared. Johnny went and stood by his side. 'Listen, Jerry, if you can shake like that and still stay up here, then you're the bravest one among us.'

'Yeah,' said Snots. 'But I agree with Enya as well.

Let's hang on a second. I'd like to know what these things are. I'd also like to know how come they haven't been seen at night. I mean, if they're as bright as this during daylight, how come they're not lighting up the hill like a bonfire once it gets dark? I think we should keep an eye on this place after nightfall, just to see what happens. We don't have to stay here or nothing, we can watch from my house. My bedroom window looks straight up here.'

As he finished speaking, a light breeze made its way up the height of ground from behind them, flirted with their hair and faces, and then was siphoned down into the Pits. It rippled through the tightly packed shafts of light, momentarily disturbing the water beneath them. And as it passed through, there rose a sound like tiny bells, the faintest of chimes.

'Man, that's weird,' said Johnny.

'Okay,' said Enya. 'I think we've been brave enough. We can go now.'

Enya turned round and faced back down the slope towards home. She came over to Jerry and took him by the hand. Johnny took Jerry's other hand, and Snots came and linked on the other side of Enya. Together they walked home, trying their best not to rush even though the fall of ground was in their favour.

They stayed at Snots's house, looking up at the Pits until it began to get dark. As the night set in, the hill became darker and darker. But with each lessening of

the light something flickered at the corner of their vision.

'They're leaving the Pits,' said Snots, 'that's the reason they don't light up the hill at night. They must only stay there during the day.'

'Yeah, but why choose there at all?' said Johnny. 'I mean, I know you'd never see them from here, 'cos they're in a hollow. But it's still out in the open. They could be seen from a plane or a helicopter *no problem*. And another thing, if they stay here then how come we see them at school all the way up in Kilfursa? And how come we saw them along the road?'

'I don't know,' said Snots. 'It could be that they just like secluded bodies of water. And maybe there's groups of them all over the place. I mean, there's little lakes and ponds up in Kilfursa as well. And maybe we've seen them along the roads because they go travelling from one place to the next. Look, lads, I think what Jimmy Pats suggested is right. I think we should go into the library in Kilfursa and look up some books on UFOs. We might find something.'

They left Snots's house soon after, Johnny and Jerry walking Enya the few doors down to her own place, and then heading off home. Jerry had become very nervous of the dark and held on to Johnny for dear life. The idea of hanging out with the big kids had suddenly lost some of its appeal. Johnny didn't say anything. He wouldn't admit it to Jerry, but he was very shaken himself. It was with relief that he opened the front door of their house, and the giving out he got from their mother for keeping Jerry out so late seemed strangely reassuring, in some way grounding him back in the ordinary, *normal* world. It was only when they were having their bedtime snack of milk and biscuits that Johnny realised that they had left their bikes behind at Enya's house. But the bikes could wait; no power on earth would make him go back out tonight.

Jerry went off to bed and slept with the light on, something he hadn't done since he was five. But the light wasn't much of a comfort to him now, because he had learnt very well that light can hide in light. So he shoved his head beneath the pillow and tried to think of something happy. What helped him fall asleep in the end was the knowledge that today he'd filled his account with a new kind of currency – karma. Karma was a good thing to go to sleep with.

Johnny stayed up for a while, trying to read, but he was too restless to concentrate. It was a book of short stories by Shaughnessy-Shaughnessy O'Shaughnessy called *The Mystery of the Empty Dog & Other Stories of the Imagination*. He'd read it all before, and had got it out just for something to do. But now he didn't have the heart for it.

Before he lay down he checked under the bed and then whipped up the pillow. Nothing. No rag dolls, no effigies. He got into the bed, his finger hesitating over

the bedside lamp. If he switched it off and then saw a shaft of light hovering in his room, he knew he'd totally freak out. He closed his eyes. The imprint of the lamp bulb lit up the inside of his lids for a few seconds, and then began to fade. With his eyes still closed, he switched off the bedside lamp. Darkness enveloped him.

court jesters without a court ...

That night, when Mr McCluskey finally fell asleep, sleep was simply a black box. However, when he woke up he found himself lying inside the sink-unit, in the cutlery drawer. The drawer was opened slightly, so that a dim shaft of moonlight penetrated into the confined space. Above his face was the corrugated roof of the draining-board. Turning on his mattress of flat knives he could see the enormous curved leg of the cork-screw risen sideways in its shallow container.

At that moment the drawer was pulled open, violently, and he was bathed in a harsh, buzzing light.

Mr McCluskey opened his eyes. He was lying in his bed, but, like an echo from his dream, the bedroom was flooded with a strange, humming light. Then, suddenly the light was gone, and the room was black. He felt thoroughly sick and disorientated.

He tried to rise from the bed, but his head was throbbing with a persistent, thrumming noise, like the sound of a generator. As his feet eventually made contact with the floor, he realised that the whole room was resonating with this sound.

He struggled forwards towards the light switch by the door, but in his confused state he ended up in the opposite direction, tangled up in the bedroom curtains. Frantically he pulled the drapes to one side, to let in the light from the street-lamps, but the street-lamps were dead, as if the whole street, not just his bedroom, was now saturated in blackness.

The noise stopped suddenly and the street-lamps came on. Mr McCluskey stood by the window, gripping the curtains with both hands, staring down into the deserted street.

At that moment he felt a popping sound inside his head, as if there had been a tremendous change in air pressure. He brought his hand to his ears, and he could feel a thin, sticky discharge against his fingers.

Finally he made it safely to the light switch. Once the light was on, the room was just an ordinary room, non-threatening, peaceful. He looked at his hands.

They were smeared with a waxy substance through which ran faint threads of blood. Mr McCluskey made his way to the bathroom, where he washed his hands and doused his face with cold water. He stayed there for a long time, just cupping handfuls of water on to his face. Finally he looked up into the mirror, his face whitened by the cold water. Then he began to dry himself with a towel, rubbing hard until the colour returned to his cheeks.

In the bedroom he struggled into some clothes. Still in his bare feet, he went downstairs to the kitchen, where he made himself a pot of strong, sweet tea. The tea brought him round, so he poured a second cup. A newspaper was on the table, *The Ballynought Review*, opened at page five and folded so that the top of the page was visible. The headline said: MYSTERY IN THE SKY DEEPENS WITH EERIE NIGHT-TIME SIGHTINGS IN KILFURSA. He had been unable to read it earlier because he had been far too sick, but he read it now.

After reading it, he could only conclude, sadly, that young Seamus Murphy and his father were well capable of destroying the deepest truth with the simplest lie. Although he knew, at the same time, that neither of them ever considered that they were lying. They were simply using their imaginations to tell stories. They were storytellers, poets, court jesters without a court. And he doubted very much that

Shaughnessy-Shaughnessy O'Shaughnessy was in any way in the least involved.

His second cup of tea finished, he poured a third, then got up and filled the kettle, putting it on to boil. He sipped from his third cup of tea, his mind and spirit reviving. But, thinking back on the day, he was suddenly surrounded by unease. The thought of being so unwell in front of his class filled him with depression. Yes, he bullied them, cajoled them, pushed them in any way he could towards the open doors of their minds, those of them that had doors, but he loved them, cared for and about them. That Coughlan boy, especially. And he remembered that, at the very moment of his collapse, it was Coughlan who had asked him if he was all right. It was Coughlan, his face awash with tears, who had gone to get Charles Chamberdale. It was Coughlan who had sought to save him.

The electric kettle gave a click to say that its water was boiled. Something in that click rescued him: perhaps simply that it was such a small, normal thing. He poured water into the teapot and brewed more tea, and in doing so felt real again. He decided that he would not go back to bed, but would find his shoes and socks and get more fully dressed.

He was determined not to spend the May bank holiday as a sick man mouldering away in his bed. This moment would be his first moment of being well.

As he poured the hot, fresh tea into the cup something caught his attention. He thought he caught a glimpse, a flicker, out of the corner of his eye. He turned to face it head-on, but it was gone.

'No,' he said out loud, 'whatever you are, you are no longer master. As long as I have a cup of tea, you are nothing.'

He lifted the cup to his lips and took a sip. Putting the cup down he began to laugh. But it wasn't the laugh of a sick man. It was the laugh of someone who has deliberately said something absurd. It was the laugh of someone *in control*.

Mr McCluskey took a second sip of tea and stood up from the kitchen table. He turned sideways and scanned the room through the edge of his vision. Wavering ribbons of light trembled through the room. He edged towards them and they moved away, grouped together. While they were together he could feel a palpable energy, something that caused him to hesitate. Together they seemed able to repel him. Apart they seemed merely to be observing him.

He took another sip of tea and sat back down at the table. Out of the corner of his eyes he could see the shafts of light dispersing through the room, as if taking up positions. It was as if, while he sat at his table sipping from his tea, he was no threat to them. And as long as that was the case, *they* were no threat to him. The secret of keeping them neutralised, therefore, was to sit back and enjoy his tea.

Mr McCluskey was beginning to feel a lot better. He believed that he was moving towards his first victory. Leaning across the table, he poured himself yet another cup of tea.

Dangerously Radioactive Hamsters ...

Enya stirred restlessly in her bed, the quilt pulled up over her face. Suddenly, the sheets under her turned into folded pages of writing. Then some invisible force stood the bed on its end and she slid down beneath the quilt. She noticed that the inside of the quilt was brown, which she was sure it had never been, and there was a clear window running down the centre. Peering through the window, she realised suddenly that she was no longer asleep in her bed but was inside a brown envelope. A brown *business envelope*. The envelope was gliding effortlessly through empty darkness, and she imagined for a moment that she must be falling inside the belly of a postbox, and that any moment now the envelope in which she was travelling would land with a slap amongst dozens of others. But through the window there suddenly came a yellow orb, throbbing with pale light, and she realised that the envelope was falling towards the moon.

Enya woke up. She rose from the bed and went to the bathroom, the details of the dream still very clear in her memory. This was the same dream she had had when she dozed off on the bus. Now that she thought about it, the dream seemed positive. It was as if she was being told that she had undergone a journey and was about to arrive at her destination. She considered that for a moment. In her dream the destination was the moon, and she knew from her reading about such things that the moon was a source of magical power.

She looked into the bathroom mirror. The night before she had soaked strips of muslin in the hawthorn soup and had gone to bed with them plastered to her face. The cloths had fallen away, no doubt tucked in among the bedclothes. But while they lay on her face they had drawn the pustules from her skin. Her spots had lost their angry redness, were beginning to dry up and heal. She knew that new ones would appear, but she no longer cared. Something about that dream had given her a new certainty, as if she now had the power she always sought. The power she had sought by tying those rags to Peggy Delaney's tree or by lighting all those candles.

She decided that instead of meeting Johnny on the school bus this morning, she would knock on his door.

After breakfast she left the house earlier than usual and walked up to the Pits. The sense of foreboding that she had felt the evening before was even stronger now that she was alone, but she overcame the urge to waver and made her way to the very top. Down in the Pits, the wafers of light were stacked as tight as they had been on her previous visit. She picked up a stone from the ground and threw it into the water. And another and another. Stone after stone fell into the ponds, making circles within circles within bigger circles. And as the water was riven with ripples, light played across its surface.

Enya stood on the lip of the pit above the disturbed water. She felt triumphant. She looked to the north, and she could see the long finger of Tip Lake glistening in the morning light. Somewhere out there she'd find Gristle Bonehead. Possibly she'd find other things as well. But now she was ready to look.

She turned from the Pits and made her way down to the houses. Out of the corners of her eyes she could see lights moving around her.

By the time Johnny got to the kitchen table this morning, his bowl of porridge had been taken over by Biggs Construction. A Biggs dumper truck floundered in the centre of the bowl, up to its cabin in soggy porridge. Tiny construction workers were drowning in the stuff. Blue plastic barrels marked *Toxic Waste* were adrift amongst the scattered bodies.

Jerry sat opposite, saying nothing, too busy layering marmalade on his toast.

Johnny picked up his spoon and began removing some of the porridge and depositing it into his mouth. He moved the spoon deliberately, in stiff-armed motions, as if he was a mechanical digger. As the porridge level dropped, so did the semblance of chaos inside the bowl. The dumper truck found its wheels touching the solid ground at the bottom. Some of the construction workers fell on their feet, and those that didn't, well, Johnny could right with the spoon. The barrels of toxic waste lay stranded, ready for pick-up. Johnny looked down into the bowl. Order had been restored and he had even managed to have his breakfast.

'Well,' said Jerry, looking up from his toast, 'for a twelve-year-old you're pretty slow on the uptake, but you've finally worked it out. You can't stop me putting crap in your breakfast, so you might as well ignore the crap and eat your breakfast anyway. Very simple really.'

At that moment the doorbell rang. The two boys were surprised when Enya walked into the kitchen.

'Your Mam left me in. What's that you're having, Jerry?'

'Toast,' said Jerry, with a practised air of sophistication.

Then Enya spotted the cereal bowl in front of Johnny and looked at it in disbelief.

'Ah, never mind him,' said Jerry, taking a bite of his toast, 'he's *always* playing with his food. He's worse than a little kid.'

'I've just come from the Pits,' said Enya.

Johnny looked shocked. 'What? On your own? What did you go there for?'

'I wanted to see if I could. If I didn't know that, then I'd be too scared to do anything else.'

Johnny looked down at the cereal bowl. He had been playing building sites with his breakfast while she was facing real danger. He felt incredibly stupid.

From the hall their mother was calling them to get ready. Within a minute the bus was outside their house, sounding its piercing blare. As they left the house Jerry shot ahead of them. He headed straight for the back of the bus, cocksure and ready to buy and sell the world.

Before he got on the bus, Johnny turned to Enya and blurted out, 'Look, that crap in my cereal bowl, Jerry puts it there every morning. It's just one of his wind-ups.'

Enya didn't seem to be listening. 'Notice anything different?' She tilted her face up to his.

Straight away Johnny saw that her spots had begun to clear up. He thought he noticed something else as well, something he couldn't quite put his finger on at first. But then it came to him.

'Yeah. You look really ... grown-up, today, Enya. And

your spots aren't as bad. That stuff from the hawthorn tree must be starting to work.'

What he said about her being grown-up surprised Enya, and she climbed the steps of the bus brimming with confidence.

As they reached the back of the bus, Snots looked up from his knitting. He had completed a leg and was now working on the seat of the pants. He would normally have begun at the waistband and worked his way down, but as this pair of trousers had started off as a scarf, he was having to work the wrong way round. But he was well used to improvising, so he just got on with it.

Enya sat down on her own next to the window and opened her schoolbag. She pulled out a book. It was called *The Yellow Wallpaper*, but Johnny couldn't quite make out the name of the author from where he was sitting.

Johnny took out a comic; it was *Dangerously Radioactive Hamsters*, one of the ones he collected.

As if not to be outdone, Jerry opened his schoolbag and produced *Animal Farm* by George Orwell. Sitting there reading it, his feet unable to touch the floor of the bus, he looked ridiculously intellectual.

Suddenly Johnny's prized comic felt totally juvenile. He rolled it up and put it back into his bag. This was going to be an extremely long bus journey.

After about twenty minutes Johnny noticed that

Enya had finished her book. She was looking at the back cover and was ready to put it away.

'Hey, Enya, could I give it a read?'

'Sure, it's really cool. I think you'll like it.'

Johnny moved nearer to her and took the book. As he did so she asked, 'What were you reading? That thing that you put in your bag?'

'Ah, that was just a comic. But I wasn't in the mood.'

'Well, let me have it, I've got nothing to do.'

Johnny fished out *Dangerously Radioactive Hamsters* and passed it, somewhat reluctantly, to Enya. She looked at the cover, stony-faced, and opened it up.

Johnny didn't dare look at her while she was reading, as he just felt too ashamed. He couldn't even concentrate on the book she'd given him, *The Yellow Wallpaper*, so he played around with it a bit, reading the back cover and then parts of the introduction, but he soon got bored until he finally decided to just read the story. It was written by someone called Charlotte Perkins Gilman and turned out to be a kind of psychological horror story about a young woman who becomes obsessed by the patterned yellow wallpaper in her room. Johnny, who had always imagined faces in the patterns of the carpet in his bedroom, got into the story very quickly.

He lost his concentration for a moment when the bus had to slow down suddenly to avoid cattle on the road. It was then that he chanced to look over at Enya, who was nearing the end of *Dangerously Radioactive Hamsters*. He noticed that she was smiling continually as she read, and from time to time would give a little giggle. When she did this she exposed her sharp yellow teeth. Teeth that Johnny thought were wonderful. Actually, it was one of the things about her that other people disliked but that Johnny found irresistible.

He was glad she had gone to the Pits by herself. He had always relied on her fearlessness. He was glad that she was still fearless. It was *her* courage that made him feel brave. And it was *her* book, now, that made him feel smart.

Snots packed away his knitting and turned to Jerry.

'What's that you're reading?' said Snots?

'Ah, it's just some kids' book about animals. But I like it 'cos the bad and nasty characters have all the fun, just like in real life. Do you know, grown-ups should be reading books like this.'

The bus had come to Kilfursa, and now began making its way through the town.

'Hey,' said Johnny, suddenly noticing, 'there aren't any more dead animals on the road today.'

'Yeah,' said Enya, 'but that might be because there's *none left*. They probably killed most of them yesterday.'

as of now, our little arrangement is over ...

Once again, Jimmy Pats was waiting for them on the pavement. He was extremely anxious to speak to Jerry.

'Jerry, if I were you I'd make myself scarce. Monkey's been enquiring for the past twenty minutes if the bus had come in yet. He wants to talk to you about something, but I have no idea what it is. You're just lucky he's gone off to the jacks.'

'Thanks for the warning,' said Jerry. 'But the truth is I don't have to worry about that dork. I can wrap him round my little finger. Anyway, he probably just wants to talk to me about this plan we have for getting back Mr Chamberdale's dog.'

'Oh yeah, and what plan is that?' asked Johnny, suddenly concerned.

'I was going to get Monkey to help me find Vigrid, 'cos I'm normally scared of dogs. But I won't be needing Monkey anymore 'cos the plan's been changed. Look, just let me handle it. I know what I'm doing.'

Jerry left everybody outside the school gates and went in to see if he could find Monkey.

'Look, Jimmy Pats, let Jerry do his stuff,' said Johnny. 'He's quite capable of looking after himself. Just have a little bit of faith. That plonker Monkey is going to be easy to deal with compared to those shafts of light. They're the *real* problem.'

'Yeah, Snots told me all about them on the phone this morning. I definitely think I should go down to Earc Luachra with you this evening. I've squared it with me Mam and Dad, and Snots says it's okay with his.'

'Then it's all settled,' said Johnny, 'you can come home with us on the school bus. We'll go off to look for Gristle, and find some way of coping with those shafts of light.'

'Man, I'm really looking forward to this. You don't know what it's like being stuck up here on my own. I feel really isolated. You lot can hang out together after school, but I've got no one. Anyway, what I was thinking for today was maybe if we all went to Kilfursa library and then to the museum. We might be able to find out something that can help us.'

'Right,' said Enya, 'everything seems to be sorted. We'll all meet at lunchtime and go to the library

together. Look, the bell's gonna go any minute and I've got a bit of sewing I need to finish. I'll see you in class.'

As she walked away, Enya began pulling the effigy of Mr Chamberdale out of her schoolbag. Johnny noticed with some surprise that she had since made a suit for it out of bits of grey flannel. It was a miniature version of the one that the real Mr Chamberdale wore.

As soon as he had entered the school yard, Jerry had headed for the jacks because that's where Jimmy Pats had said Monkey was. He found Monkey outside, leaning against the wall, smoking.

'I heard you were looking for me,' said Jerry.

'I thought it fair to tell you,' started Monkey, 'on account of the fact that you're just a stupid little kid, that I'm going to let you off the hook. As of now, our little arrangement is over. I'm releasing you from it.'

Jerry looked at Monkey coldly. 'What are you talking about? You're not making sense.'

'What I'm talking about,' said Monkey, 'is that you no longer have to set up your brother. I'm not interested anymore; I've got bigger fish to fry. This was on the school noticeboard this morning ... '

Monkey pulled a folded sheet of paper from his back pocket and handed it to Jerry. Jerry unfolded it as soon as he had it in his hand. It was a notice in very large print.

REWARD:

A SUM OF FORTY EURO WILL BE PRESENTED TO ANYONE WHO CAN CAN SUCCESSFULLY RETURN VIGRID TO MY OFFICE.

The notice was signed: *Mr C. Chamberdale.*

'We had a deal,' said Jerry. 'I was going to come up with a plan and you were going to help me catch Vigrid. You agreed.'

'Yeah,' said Monkey. 'But now I don't need your plan. I'm going to find Vigrid on my own. Anyway, he's obviously up here somewhere near Kilfursa, probably out in the woods. I'll find him on my own during the weekend. Now, pog off.'

Jerry looked at Monkey with contempt. The truth was, he was glad to be released from their agreement, but he wasn't going to let Monkey know that.

'I want you to know,' said Jerry, 'that I'm very disappointed in you. A deal is a deal. You might live to regret breaking it.'

'What are you going to do, send me a solicitor's letter? Go on, you little maggot, pog off!'

Jerry turned round and walked off, feigning a huff. In reality he was delighted. '*Moron*,' he muttered under his breath. At that moment the bell rang for the start of school.

Jerry made his way through the school yard. Kids were rushing to their different classes, hauling schoolbags, their faces filled with either anxiety or

boredom. Well, Jerry would never be anxious or bored. Not about school, anyway. He was in control. He was smart enough to follow lessons and keep up with his homework, and he was smart enough to enjoy it. No, you wouldn't find Jerry rushing *anywhere*. As he looked at all the anxious, worried little faces, Jerry felt very satisfied with himself. Things were good. Having karma in the bank was much better than money. That was something Monkey would *never* understand.

consider yourself definitely detained ...

When Mr McCluskey's class turned up outside the room, they found the door wide open and Mr Chamberdale sitting at Mr McCluskey's desk. This was a surprise, as most of them were expecting Mrs Dooley. He motioned everyone in as they appeared outside the door, and very soon they were all at their desks. Monkey was the last one in, and Chamberdale told him to shut the door behind him.

Monkey was feeling very pleased with himself. He

had this very strong feeling that the reward of forty euro had his name on it. As Monkey took his seat Jimmy Pats looked at him.

'Did you get to talk to Jerry?' asked Jimmy Pats, deciding it might do him good to be friendly.

Monkey gave Jimmy Pats a lopsided grin and the thumbs-up sign.

Jimmy Pats was taken by surprise, because Monkey wouldn't normally do this, and, half by reflex, he found himself acknowledging the signal, giving a thumbs-up in return.

Mr Chamberdale noticed, and looked at the two carefully, making a mental note to remember this exchange. Experience had taught him that it was always useful to determine all the different alliances in any given classroom. He recognised Monkey as being the boy who had come before him the day before, and assumed that these two must be the best of friends.

Jimmy Pats sat back in his chair, his analytical mind doing its usual work. As he began to think about it, Monkey's happy demeanour could have many different interpretations. It could simply mean *It's okay, I saw Jerry, thanks for asking*; or, on the other hand, it could mean that Monkey was happy because he'd pulled a fast one on Jerry, and by extention on Johnny and the rest of the gang. As Jimmy Pats thought about it he became increasingly paranoid, and Monkey's cheerful thumbs-up began to take on

sinister connotations. Having an analytical mind is not always a good thing.

Mr Chamberdale noticed that Jimmy Pats Murphy had undergone a change in composure. The boy looked suddenly preoccupied and troubled. This was very strange indeed, because only a moment before he had been exchanging triumphant signals with his friend. Mr Chamberdale was beginning to wonder, therefore, if this was perhaps a prelude to some kind of trouble. He decided to keep an eye on the pair of them for the duration of the lesson.

The Principal cleared his throat in order to get everybody's attention. In the clear morning light of the classroom he looked stern and imposing. His bald head shone and his warts seemed to tremble as he moved his face to speak. His sad, blue eyes commanded you to look into them and become melancholy. But it was a stupefying kind of thing, making you feel you were becoming drowsy. You would find yourself totally under his command, quietened by his blue eyes.

'Good morning, class. As you are aware I am Mr Chamberdale, and I will be taking Mr McCluskey's class while he's away, which looks very much like it will be for only one day. Mr McCluskey phoned me this morning from his home and, you will be very glad to hear, he is much recovered. I remember how you were all so upset yesterday. He feels that taking today off, coupled with the long weekend, will give him time enough to recuperate fully. He should be back to you on Tuesday.'

Mr Chamberdale sat forward in his chair, his palms and fingers together as if praying. He gathered his thoughts before continuing.

'Lest I forget,' said Mr Chamberdale, 'today's lunchbreak will be extended by half an hour due to a short staff meeting after lunch. But that's *thirty minutes*, not *thirty-one* minutes. Make sure you get back here on time, all of you. And now, very briefly, I would like to explain a few things before we start the lesson. Mr McCluskey came down with a very unusual strain of Oriental 'flu that gave him a fever and made him delirious. That's why he behaved the way he did yesterday. As for the things you experienced in this room yesterday afternoon with Mrs Dooley, well, certain things happen at this time of the year, mainly to do with the position of the earth in relation to the sun. This causes strange atmospheric results, such as lights in the sky, which I'm sure you read about in the local newspaper. What you saw in the classroom yesterday with Mrs Dooley was simply a natural phenomenon. It's a bit like an eclipse and there's nothing to worry about. Actually, it was all a bit of fun, wasn't it? Mrs Dooley told me how you had all enjoyed yourselves, and she was laughing when we discovered what had caused it all. We had some experts from the

local council come in and inspect this classroom, but they found it to be quite clear. That's because the position of the sun had changed in the sky by then, and those funny things couldn't happen anymore.'

Mr Chamberdale rose from his desk and went over to the window. 'Now, I want you all to remain in your seats while I close the blinds and demonstrate that the room is back to normal. When the blinds are closed I want you all to shut your eyes, just like you did yesterday with Mrs Dooley. And when you shut your eyes you'll see that everything is as normal as it should be. You'll just be in darkness.'

Mr Chamberdale closed the blinds and everyone in the class shut their eyes.

Just before he had shut his, Johnny had seen Jimmy Pats and Snots exchange a sceptical look; Mr Chamberdale wasn't fooling *them*. But in one respect, the Principal was right; with their eyes closed, the class could see nothing. Johnny scanned the room out of the corner of his eye, but the shafts of light were nowhere to be seen.

Mr Chamberdale drew back the blinds and the room was filled with sunlight once more. Then he opened a few of the windows. The faint sound of traffic could be heard, and a breeze came in the window and shook the blinds, lifting the charts and maps on the wall beside the blackboard, so that for a brief moment they flapped about. The room was a normal schoolroom.

'Now, class,' said Mr Chamberdale, 'I think it is about time we got down to the business of school, wouldn't you agree? Let's see, according to Mr McCluskey's notes against the register, both Johnny Coughlan and Enya Murphy are marked down for detention during lunchtime today for failure to do their maths homework. So I'll see you both here at lunchtime.'

Johnny had totally forgotten about the detention. That meant that their plans to visit the library with the rest of the gang would be upset. Johnny thought about it for a second. He knew from experience that Chamberdale could be reasonable, so he decided to have a go.

'Excuse me, sir, but we can't be at detention today, sir. We've got something we have to do, something educational. But we're both prepared to do the detention after the holiday instead, sir.'

Chamberdale looked Johnny straight in the eye. 'If you would both like to do detention after the holiday as well, that can easily be arranged. But you are definitely in detention today, Coughlan. Consider yourself definitely detained.'

Johnny realised that to argue would be a mistake. So he decided to agree.

'Yes, sir. Sorry, sir.'

Mr Chamberdale looked down at his desk and something caught his eye. It was the dried-out paper

hanky that Mr McCluskey had taken from Johnny. Chamberdale put his hands into his pockets and removed a tweezers. With the tweezers he lifted the soiled paper tissue and got up from his desk. Then he made his way towards Johnny.

Johnny watched him coming and decided that whatever happened he would try to remain calm. But by the time Chamberdale had reached his desk, Johnny was filled with disquiet. The Principal lifted the hanky close to Johnny's face.

'Would I be totally mistaken, young Coughlan, if I was to say that I'd seen this dirty handkerchief before?'

Johnny knew that there was one thing that he mustn't do. He mustn't lie. Well, he could lie a bit, but he'd have to be careful. Chamberdale was obviously sharper than Mr McCluskey. And that was very sharp indeed.

'Actually, sir, you're absolutely right, sir. When I came back from seeing you the other day Mr McCluskey wanted a report of the whole thing, and when I told him, he asked me to take out the paper hanky, sir. And when I did he put it on his desk and said: "*Class, I want you all to look at this tissue. This tissue is a perfect example of how we can get caught out by the smallest details. Coughlan here left this tissue by the side of the road very early this morning, in a place sixteen kilometres from here, and, yet, here is this same tissue, accusing Coughlan of all his wrongdoings. I want to leave this tissue on my desk to remind you all of the hazards of doing the wrong thing in the wrong place at the wrong hour of the morning.'"*

Mr Chamberdale looked around the class. He was searching for the most innocent face there. His gaze came upon Snots, who was looking up at him with a bubble of snot hanging from his left nostril. Chamberdale knew that Snots was not the one.

Then his face fell upon Julie Hegarty. Julie Hegarty looked genuinely angelic. Most of the boys were secretly and hopelessly in love with her. Even Johnny, at one time, had been in love with her. But that was before he met Enya. Julie Hegarty was beautiful. She was also pure. She had a highly refined sense of right and wrong. She was incapable of lying. She was incapable of doing anything bad. And Mr Chamberdale could tell.

'What's your name, young lady?' asked Chamberdale.

'Julie Hegarty, sir.'

'Well, Julie, I want you to tell me something,' and he held the handkerchief up by the tweezers, 'is this true?'

Johnny felt time and space lose all meaning. He was about to fall into a Black Hole. A dirty great Black Hole.

Julie Hegarty looked at the tissue. And because Julie Hegarty was honest, and good, and pure, something

happened that Mr Chamberdale could not suspect. Julie Hegarty had a dilemma.

She knew that Johnny was lying, to the extent that not a single thing he had said was the truth. However, she had been asked a misleading question. For Mr Chamberdale had shown her the dirty handkerchief, and had asked her if *that* was true. And the handkerchief on its own *was* true. It told no lies. It presented itself as it was, and no more. So Julie decided to tell the truth as she saw it without having to make the decision as to what question she had *actually* been asked.

'Well, sir, I can tell you exactly what happened, sir.'

'Please do,' said Mr Chamberdale.

Johnny held his breath. He knew he was dead. Julie Hegarty did not lie.

'Well, sir,' said Julie, 'Johnny took it out of his pocket and Mr McCluskey asked him what it was and when Johnny told him Mr McCluskey was very impressed. And the main reason Mr McCluskey put it on the desk, sir, was because he thought it was beautiful.'

'Beautiful, did you say?'

'Yes, sir. He thought it was beautiful, sir.'

Now, the thing is, Julie had told the absolute truth, without going into any detail. Which was just as well, because it's the details that always complicate things. But Mr Chamberdale, because he could tell that she *was* telling the truth, jumped to the conclusion that what she was telling him was also *exactly* what Johnny had told him.

'Yes, I can see what he meant. Yes, yes. It *is* quite beautiful, really, to think that somebody's wrongdoing can be uncovered by something as seemingly insignificant as a dirty handkerchief. I hope you've learned your lesson from this, young Coughlan.'

'Oh yes, sir,' said Johnny, breathing with relief.

'Well,' said Chamberdale, 'I'd say that everybody has got the point now, so we can put this disgusting piece of rubbish into the bin. What do you think, Coughlan?'

'Oh yes, sir, definitely into the bin, sir. That's the place for it, sir.'

Mr Chamberdale walked back to the front of the class and deposited the dirty tissue in the bin. It was the end of quite a career for that particular dirty tissue, for very few dirty tissues get to come back from the dead, as that one had, twice. Johnny watched it parachute into the bin, and hoped that he'd never see it again.

'Well now, young Coughlan,' said Mr Chamberdale, turning back to face the class, 'tell me, how are your maths, Coughlan?'

Johnny thought: *No more lies*.

'Actually, sir, not very good, sir. I don't really like maths, sir. I have difficulty understanding them, Mr Chamberdale.'

Mr Chamberdale looked at Johnny with intense pity. It was the wrong answer.

Mr Chamberdale spent the entire lesson trying to make maths easy to understand, and checking at every instant that Johnny was understanding him. Johnny had never worked so hard in his life. By the time the bell rang for the first break, Johnny's brain was completely frazzled.

a homicidal ping-pong bat ...

Oh, man, that was a nightmare,' said Johnny to Enya as they left the classroom.

But Enya wasn't listening. Enya was mad at Johnny. Enya was mad at Johnny because it was Julie Hegarty who had got him off the hook. Enya had begun to imagine that maybe there was some kind of *feeling* there. Unfortunately, Johnny didn't even know that she was mad at him, so when she laid a trap to see if he was guilty of something, he fell right into it.

'That was really good of Julie not to shop you to Chamberdale,' said Enya sweetly.

'Yeah, wasn't it just,' said Johnny. And then he recalled that moment of panic that he had had, just before Julie answered Chamberdale's question, and a note of intense gratitude entered into his voice. 'Wow, she really saved my life. I think I should thank her.'

'Saved your life, did she, you ungrateful brat! And how many times have *I* saved your life? How come you didn't thank *me*?' She gave Johnny the most almighty thump into the muscle of his right arm.'

'Hey, what the hell's that for?'

'I saw you looking at her in class, Johnny. Your mouth was wide open. You still fancy her. *Admit it!*' and she gave him a second thump, this time into the muscle of his left arm.

'Ow, take it easy, you're gonna cripple me! I was looking at her in class 'cos I thought she'd tell the truth and I'd be finished, and if my mouth was wide open it's because I was terrified. Ah, come on, Enya, this is crazy. You know you're my girlfriend.'

Enya went to give Johnny another thump. He ducked low and she got him straight in the mouth. He didn't like this at all. He was beginning to hurt very badly and he had no way of persuading her that he was innocent. He was therefore very relieved when Enya stormed off in a huff. His lip was beginning to feel numb. And so were his two arms.

Meanwhile, Jimmy Pats Murphy was trying to get past Monkey in the corridor. But Monkey wanted to have a word. Monkey looked very pleased with himself and this, in itself, was disturbing enough.

'What did you give me the thumbs-up for, you little slimeball? You're no friend of mine,' said Monkey, mustering as much bad attitude as he could.

Jimmy Pats was beginning to quake. Monkey was one of the school bullies and he obviously felt in a bullying mood.

'But, Monkey,' said Jimmy Pats, 'you gave me the thumbs-up first. I was just returning the compliment.'

'It wasn't meant as a compliment. It just meant that I'd done my business with that little maggot, Jerry Coughlan. And don't you ever call me Monkey again. What, do I look like a gorilla or something?'

'No, of course not,' said Jimmy Pats, thinking to himself: *You look more like a baboon*.

'Then don't call me that name ever again. Otherwise you're *dead*,' said Monkey, giving Jimmy Pats a jab in the arm that nearly crippled him.

Man, what a moron! thought Jimmy Pats as he went off down the corridor, his arm throbbing.

After the break everyone went back to their classes. Mr Chamberdale noticed that when Jimmy Pats came in he was rubbing his arm. He seemed in pain. And when Johnny came in he noticed that he was rubbing *both* his arms and that he had a fat lip. Chamberdale walked over to where Johnny was sitting. 'And what happened to you, young Coughlan?'

'What do you mean, sir?' said Johnny. There was no way he wanted everybody to know that his girlfriend could knock strips off him. It would be just too embarrassing. And the other thing was, he didn't want Enya to get into trouble. He'd never do that to her, because, and here was the funny thing, he was pleased that she had been jealous of Julie Hegarty. It proved she still loved him.

'Well, it's obvious to everyone that you've been in a fight,' said Chamberdale.

'No, sir, I haven't been in a fight, sir. I fell down the stairs, sir.'

Mr Chamberdale said nothing but turned back and walked to where Jimmy Pats was sitting, a few desks ahead and to the left of Johnny.

'And tell me, it's Jimmy Pats Murphy, isn't it?' said Mr Chamberdale, and Jimmy nodded. 'So, tell me, Jimmy Pats Murphy, did you fall down the stairs as well?'

'Eh ... no, sir,' said Jimmy Pats, telling the truth. However, the question had surprised him so much that he had hesitated, and his answer sounded unconvincing.

'What I think,' said Mr Chamberdale, 'is that you two have been fighting.'

'But we haven't, sir, we're best friends, sir,' protested Johnny.

'It's true, sir, we're best friends, sir,' said Jimmy Pats,

so confused by what was happening that there was an anxious edge to his voice. He was unnerved by the whole thing. What the *hell* was Chamberdale talking about?

'*Don't argue with me*,' said Mr Chamberdale. There was a sharp finality in his voice that forbade any type of contradiction.

'Jimmy Pats Murphy, it is quite obvious to me that you have been fighting with Coughlan during the first break. You will join us in detention, Jimmy Pats Murphy, at lunchtime. Now, everybody, get out your history textbooks and turn to page seventy-three.'

Monkey had been following this with extreme interest. He sat up in his chair, grinning his head off. While he'd been accosting Jimmy Pats earlier, he had heard Enya and Johnny having their row, and knew that Enya was to blame for Johnny's injuries. And to think that Johnny was getting the blame for belting Jimmy Pats in the arm, when all along it had been Monkey himself, was just priceless. Monkey looked over at Coughlan and shot him a self-satisfied smile. The next fifty minutes was the toughest history lesson that Johnny and Jimmy Pats had ever gone through. Mr Chamberdale was merciless. He badgered the pair of them with questions as if he was a homicidal ping-pong bat and they were the unfortunate balls.

By the end of the lesson Johnny was feeling extremely unwell, but he had to stay where he was because he had detention. Monkey turned to Jimmy Pats and gave him the lop-sided grin and the thumbs-up, and then he threw his eyes over in the direction of Johnny. Jimmy Pats was livid. As the class left the room, Mr Chamberdale reminded them of the half-hour extension to the break.

After everyone except the three detainees had left, Mr Chamberdale went over and closed the door. Then he returned to his desk and sat down. He noticed that Enya had her hand up.

'Yes, Miss Murphy, what is it?' asked the Principal with impatience. He'd had a solid morning of classes and wasn't in the mood to stay behind with these three delinquents.

'I'm sorry, sir, I don't mean to contradict you, sir, but Jimmy Pats shouldn't be here, sir. He wasn't in a fight with Johnny, sir. I was.'

Mr Chamberdale looked at her in disbelief. He noticed that Johnny had tears welling up in his eyes, the second time he'd seen him upset in the one week.

'My God, what the blazes did you do to him?'

'She didn't mean it, sir,' said Johnny.

'Be quiet, Coughlan! I'll hear one person at a time. Carry on, Miss Murphy.'

'It's very embarrassing, sir, but it's a kinda girl-boy thing. I thought Johnny was interested in another girl, but he wasn't. I know that now, I can see it in his face. But I was upset, sir. So I just snapped. And Johnny took

181

it 'cos he'd never hit a girl, sir.' There was a little quiver in her voice, now, but she sat bolt upright in her chair.

Mr Chamberdale looked at her solemnly. He was experienced enough to know that she was actually telling the truth and he was amazed by her honesty. He looked over at Johnny, who had turned a bright shade of beetroot pink, and then he turned to Jimmy Pats.

'And tell me, Mr Murphy, why were you rubbing your arm when you came into class?'

'A football thumped into me in the playground, sir. Someone had kicked it really hard and I was in the way. It still hurts, sir,' said Jimmy Pats.

Mr Chamberdale sat back in his chair and looked down at the desk. He wasn't absolutely certain that Jimmy Pats was telling the truth, but his story was plausible enough. However, he felt, beyond a shadow of doubt, that he hadn't been fighting with Coughlan. He looked up from the desk.

'Well, now, Coughlan and Miss Murphy, this is the second time this week that you've demonstrated an unwavering and honourable loyalty to each other and to your friends. And I'm not talking about that stupid kind of loyalty that one so often witnesses in schools. You impress me, all of you. But only in regard to your *characters*, not your *schoolwork*. And let me tell you, not too far in the future you'll be *in my part* of the school, and your classwork had *better show a marked improvement*. I will be watching you very closely.'

Mr Chamberdale looked at the three of them sternly, a steely glint in his eyes reinforcing his message. Then he squared his shoulders, cleared his throat and continued.

'Now, as to the matter of this detention – it was deserved and you should do it. However, I have received a favourable report that inclines me towards leniency. I had a phonecall from Peggy Delaney of Earc Luachra. She was singing your praises and explained that you had apologised to her for your earlier behaviour. She also informed me that yesterday afternoon you took the trouble to bury a dead badger that had been killed on the road. In her opinion you acted very thoughtfully and she wanted me to know about it. So, I'm going to use this as a reason, and a very good reason, I think, to let you off your detention. You can go, the three of you. But let me warn you: I expect you to work very hard at your lessons for the rest of the day. And I'll make sure that you do.'

let's examine the facts ...

Outside in the corridor Enya was rummaging through her schoolbag. Finally she brought out the effigy she was working on. Jimmy Pats looked at it in astonishment. It was obviously a likeness of Mr Chamberdale, even down to the warts on his face, which were made from tiny bobbles of pink thread.

'My God, Enya, that isn't a voodoo doll, is it? It looks just like him,' said Jimmy Pats.

'Yeah, it's a voodoo doll, all right. But it's not what you think. This is to do good, and I'm really glad that I made it. It's to cure his warts. That old Chamberdale is a good sort, really.'

'So, how does it work?' asked Jimmy Pats.

'It works very slowly, one wart at a time,' said Enya, taking a small embroidery scissors from her bag. With a snip of the scissors she removed one of the pink bobbles, which fell to the floor. As she did this she muttered a spell under her breath: *'One snip of a wart, and the wart is nought.'*

'Cool,' said Jimmy Pats.

Enya put the effigy back in her bag. 'That's enough for now,' she said. 'You've got to do one wart a day, otherwise it won't work. It can't be rushed.'

As soon as she had the doll back in her bag, she looked up at Johnny. She put her hand on his shoulder.

'Johnny, I'm sorry about that battering I gave you.'

At this, Jimmy Pats felt a bit uncomfortable. 'Hey, lads, I'm going on ahead. I'll see you at the library.'

After Jimmy Pats had left, Enya and Johnny made their way slowly through the school building, not really saying that much. But Johnny had forgiven her and Enya knew it. They walked side by side, taking their time.

By the time Johnny and Enya made it to the library, Jimmy Pats was already there and in consultation with Snots and Jerry. Snots gave them the update.

'There's not much we can find out here, after all. We've looked through most of the UFO books and found out two similarities with what's happening here in Kilfursa and Earc Luachra. First of all, in a lot of places UFOs are very active over large bodies of water, like lakes. Nobody seems to know why, but they are. The other thing is kinda funny. If you read most of these books, and I'm talking about the ones written by actual witnesses, they all make the writers look stupid. They write down stuff that happened to them but it's

almost always silly stuff. And it makes *them* look silly. And it makes these *books* look silly. And that's why people don't take UFOs seriously. But if we told people what's been happening here, it would sound silly too, wouldn't it? All those delusions we were having, and everything. Well, when you read all these other cases in the books there seems to be a pattern. All the stuff that *could* be real gets gobbled up in the silly stuff. And I think that's what's happening here.'

'Wait a minute,' said Enya. 'I'm confused. Say all that again, slowly. But this time try to make sense.'

'Okay,' said Snots, patiently. 'Well, this is the way I see it. First of all, most of the stuff that's happened to us isn't real at all; only a little bit of it. Like, say, the shafts of light. The shafts of light are real. Okay, so far? Well, how about this: all that other stuff might just be put inside our minds by the shafts of light to confuse us. I'm talking about those visions we were having of police cars that weren't there, and those weird thoughts we were getting in the classroom – I don't know about you, but during Mr McCluskey's lessons yesterday I thought I'd solved the mystery of the universe. I even drew a picture of what it looked like. But when I looked at it afterwards it was just a straight line with a squiggle in the middle.'

'But why would the shafts of light want to confuse us? What's the point?' asked Enya, trying to follow each bit as she went along.

'Because,' continued Snots, getting into his stride, 'if we're confused by the shafts of light, then we can't deal with them properly. It's like a weapon they use, to make us stupid so we can't fight. And another reason could be this: they don't want people to be *sure* they exist, because then people might be able to wipe them out or stop them, so they make their *very existence* look ridiculous. That's the perfect camouflage. I mean, look at *The Ballynought Review*. The reporters think it's just a laugh, so they don't bother to investigate it properly. And who do we rely on to give us accurate information? Reporters and newspapers, that's who. The same goes for the police. They don't take it seriously so they won't investigate. It's all done on purpose.'

'Snots is right,' said Jimmy Pats. 'And I have another theory. Everyone says that UFOs and lights in the sky come from outer space and they're aliens. But what if that is just an illusion as well? We *believe* it comes from space, and because we believe that, we'll be looking in the wrong direction entirely. What if the lights are caused by something that lives on Earth, something that's always lived here? Like some gigantic but invisible creature that gets its kicks from messing around with our minds? If you think about it, it's no more far-fetched than UFOs.'

Jimmy Pats took out his notebook. 'Let's examine the facts,' he said, flipping over a few pages. 'We know

that, whatever it is, it has an effect on animals. It's been driving most of the wildlife mental. And what's happened to all the dogs? We know about the shafts of light, and we know that they live on the water down in the Pits. We also know that there's a lot more water down in Earc Luachra, in other words: Tip Lake. And we have to go to Tip Lake anyway to be able to find Enya's crocodile. So that's what we should do. Forget all this UFO stuff. It's just a red herring.'

'Well,' said Johnny, 'I think I follow what you're saying. As long as we remember that this is all just a *theory*. First we have to prove it all to ourselves. And you're right, we should concentrate on what we know and all go down to Tip Lake. We can show Jimmy Pats the Pits this afternoon, and we can do Tip Lake tomorrow, when we've got loads of time and plenty of daylight. So, what are we doing now, then? Is it back to school or what?'

'Nah,' said Jerry. 'We've got an extra half-hour, so we might as well use it. And besides, Snots and Jimmy Pats want us to go to the museum. They reckon we might find something there that could help us.'

'Like what?' said Johnny.

'Like local history stuff,' said Jimmy Pats. 'There's not much information in the library on local history, but there is down at the museum. Who knows, maybe something like this happened in the area before? And if it did, there should be a record of it. We might even be able to find out how they dealt with it. It's long shot, but you never know. I'll go on ahead and see what I can find. I'll be upstairs in the museum library. In the meantime you can get me some chips 'cos I haven't had any lunch and I'm starving. I'll settle up with you at the museum.'

a collection of ears ...

When they got to the chipper, Johnny was half-hoping that Jerry would pay for the lot in order to increase his karma, but it didn't happen. They each paid for their own, plus another with extra salt and vinegar for Jimmy Pats, and set off for the museum.

The Kilfursa Museum and Cultural Centre was a bit further down from the library, and was housed in the old bottling works. The Kilfursa Bottle Company had gone bust sometime towards the end of the 1960s, caving in to the competition from the city suppliers, but up to that time it had made bottles for almost everyone in the Irish drinks trade. Their main

customer was Guinness's, but they also made bottles for the various soft drinks suppliers throughout the greater Ballynought area. After the company went into liquidation, the building was taken over by the local council, who turned it into a museum.

The ground floor was devoted to 'cultural glass', which, in Kilfursa terms translated as a collection of empty beer bottles. There were nearly a hundred display cases containing excellent examples of cultural glass in the larger part of the exhibition area, but there were one or two exhibits that had absolutely nothing to do with glass whatsoever. Johnny's favourite was the meteorite, which was in a reinforced cabinet against the far wall as you came in the main entrance. He loved it because it had a very personal connection with his chosen author. Every time he visited the museum he would pay his respects to the meteorite and this time was no exception.

The meteorite, a black, bubbled fragment of rock the size of a walnut, sat on a small plinth in the glass cabinet. Its surface was glossy, almost waxen. There was a history of the meteorite printed on laminated board on the back wall of the cabinet. Under the heading, FRAGMENT FROM THE FAMOUS *WOLD NEWTON METEOR*, it read:

This is a fragment from the famous meteor that landed on the 13th of December, 1795, in Wold Newton in the East Riding of Yorkshire, England. The impact was witnessed by the passengers and drivers of two passing coaches, which contained learned men and women from Europe and America who were present on business. On reaching the impact site they agreed to divide the meteorite amongst themselves, and the coachmen were dispatched to the nearest farmhouse for a heavy hammer. The meteorite was duly smashed and the fragments divided between the passengers and the coachmen. In later research it was found that the descendants of those travellers had all achieved prominence in the arts, many becoming eminent writers and poets. It has been speculated that immediately after impact the meteorite gave off radioactive emissions that altered the genetic structure of those exposed to it that caused intellectual mutations in succeeding generations. The extant fragments that have been tested, including this one, now appear free of any radioactivity.

The meteorite pieces were passed down through the generations as a family heirloom, and at least two Irish writers are known to have had fragments, namely Fitz-James O'Brien and Oscar Wilde. The fragment in this museum was donated by the science-fiction writer Shaughnessy-Shaughnessy O'Shaughnessy, a descendant of Fitz-James O'Brien; he also inherited a second fragment, passed down from his mother's family, who were descended from the American writer H. P. Lovecraft. Mr O'Shaughnessy lives locally in the Ballynought district.

Johnny put his forehead against the glass of the cabinet, hoping that some kind of emanations, *any kind of emanations*, would pass from the meteorite into

his brain. Johnny had secret ambitions to be a rock'n'roll poet and science-fiction writer, just like his hero Shaughnessy-Shaughnessy O'Shaughnessy, and daydreamed that he could be transformed by regular exposure to the meteorite.

While Johnny was bathing his brain in imaginary radioactivity, everybody else had gone up the stairs to the museum library. Johnny lingered for another minute, looking at the exhibits and eating chips from his pocket. The consumption of food was strictly forbidden inside the museum, so all the gang had poured their chips into their jacket pockets, from where they could be taken out surreptitiously and eaten.

Johnny wasn't really interested in the 'cultural glass' exhibits, but he wanted a bit of a break from Enya and the others. His swollen lip, where Enya had whacked him, was becoming sore, and this was made worse by the vinegar he'd put on his chips. He was feeling a bit down.

To tell the truth, most of the exhibits, with the exception of the meteorite and a collection of ears gathered by the late Captain Thomas O'Breen, were quite boring. The 'cultural glass' section housed a collection of three thousand empty bottles, among which were the three bottles found inside the stomach of the pike that bit off the arm of Fr Enda Murphy. But, as all the bottles looked the same, nobody, including the museum staff, knew which were the famous three, so the whole thing was incredibly boring to look at. Perhaps that is why the local pub, *The Injured Priest*, owned by Jimmy Pats's father, received more visits from tourists than the museum.

Johnny took a pickled onion from his pocket, which made his lip sting like mad, and looked through Captain Thomas O'Breen's collection of ears. Suddenly, as he gazed into the glass case he could see Enya's reflection. She was standing behind him.

'Johnny, what's keeping you? Jimmy Pats has found something in the archives of the local paper. They've got copies of the paper going back to when it was started in 1873. You should come up and see it. Hey, you okay?'

'Just wanted a break,' said Johnny, putting a chip into his mouth and wincing as the salt stung his lip. 'Here, have a pickled onion,' he added, taking one out of his pocket, 'and let's go upstairs.'

In the museum library the others were leaning over a newspaper spread out on a sloping table.

'Here, Johnny,' said Jimmy Pats, 'have a look at this. It's from *The Ballynought Review* of 1922. I think it might be a description of the same thing that's happening now.'

The article was headlined: ARCHDEACON SEEKS INSTRUCTION ON ANGELS, and went as follows:

Clergyman novelist, Archdeacon Maurice Bartholomew Murphy, is seeking advice from his Bishop in Kilcairn over the recent sightings of angels over the waters of Tip Lake.

Parishioners of Earc Luachra, on Tip's southern shore, have reported seeing angels hovering over the lake for most of the month of June. The best time to see the angels, according to local informants, is between the hours of eleven at night and six-thirty in the morning.

Eileen Drooney-Murphy of Earc Luachra West saw one of the angels this past Sunday: 'I'd just fed the scraps to the dogs, scattered them in the yard, when I saw a light from the corner of my eye. When I looked again I could see three very large men hanging from the sky on wings of spun gold. Each man was as wide as a cow and as tall as a hayrick. They floated in the one place for the longest time and then flew off north along the lake towards Rushy Island. I called my husband and my mother out from the house, and they saw it too.'

Similar sightings have been described just north of Kilfursa Town, near Lizard's Ear East. Locals there have spoken of angels entering into the ground. After all such sightings the fields have been dutifully inspected, but no evidence of anything unusual has yet been uncovered.

Local opinion is divided as to whether the area should be blessed or exorcised. Some people are describing it as a sign from God, and others the work of the devil. Archdeacon Murphy, acting Parish Priest of Earc Luachra North, has written to Bishop William Ryle-Murphy seeking advice on what course of action he should take.

Readers will recall that Archdeacon Murphy was in the news last year when his fourth novel, Tunnels of the Moon, a Romance of the Fantastic, *was published in London.*

Johnny read the article in silence, munching the last of his chips. Swap angels for UFOs and the stories were pretty much the same. However, what really intrigued him in the article was the reference to Archdeacon Murphy. The Archdeacon was one of the literary heroes of Ballynought, a kind of precursor to Shaughnessy-Shaughnessy O'Shaughnessy. He was also related to Johnny on his mother's side. Murphy's novels were written in a very careful, old-fashioned style, and Johnny had only ever managed to read one of them all the way through to the end. It was called *The Woman at the Wave-Mouth*. He had never heard of the one mentioned in the article, and decided that he would call into the town library on the way back to school to see if they had it.

'I think this is important,' said Snots. 'It not only proves that what is happening now has happened before, but that everyone survived it. So it's not necessarily the end of the world, I mean, now that it's happening again.'

Enya wasn't too convinced of the merits of this argument. 'So? You probably wouldn't die if you caught worms, but you'd still have the worms.'

'Jeeze, lads,' said Johnny, looking at his watch for the first time in ages. 'We're due back in about two minutes. We better get a move on.'

On the way up the road they passed the library and Johnny sent the others on ahead. He went in and

enquired about *Tunnels of the Moon*. The librarian found an old hardback copy for him and he took it out on his ticket.

an ant would knock him down ...

By the time Johnny pushed open the door to the classroom, he was already five minutes late. Mr Chamberdale wasn't at all happy. He had specifically warned everybody to be punctual after the extended lunch.

Johnny decided it was best to get in first and simply to give his apology before one was demanded of him. After saying sorry for disrupting the lesson, Johnny explained what had kept him late. Mr Chamberdale perked up a bit at the mention of the book. As coincidence would have it, they had just started an English lesson, and he instructed Johnny to read from the opening of the Archdeacon's novel.

Johnny sat at his desk and opened the first page. He began to read, faltering a bit to begin with, but then getting into his stride. The opening sentence was long and complicated, and Johnny crawled through it carefully, like a man getting used to the dark. The class listened intently, trying to make it out. The book began:

> *Call me Jonah, for that is my name, and hear my tale of a boy who left his home and his family to become a cabin-boy aboard* The Water's Mercy, *thus apprenticing himself to the shifting whims of the sea, until a greater force carried him to a world beyond the one he had known. And start with me, as I started then, in those years long ago when I was but twelve years old, setting foot on board ship for the first time, bound to a life of hard work and mean days, of dry biscuits riddled with mealworm, and adventures to places more distant than the mind can easily imagine.*

After reading for a while, Johnny became easy with the long sentences and discovered that the trick was to say everything slowly. The more deliberately he spoke, the more sense it made. The story centred on a boy, the same age as himself, who leaves home in the year 1851 to become a ship's cabin-boy. One day his ship is caught in a storm somewhere west of the Americas and is sucked up into the swirling winds of a hurricane. From there, the ship is forced into an airborne channel of water that stretches between the earth and the moon. After a voyage of many weeks, the ship eventually reaches the moon and is cast upon its surface. The moon of the novel is a place not of water, but of shifting sands so liquid that the ship travels

along the surface with ease. Just as their supplies are about to run out, the ship comes upon an island towering out of the sands. The island appears deserted but it is riddled with caves, and the ship's crew descend through the caves and into the very heart of the moon itself. And it is there that the story really begins, telling the fantastic adventures of the crew.

As the tale unfolded the class listened with more and more interest – even Orla Daly, who was drawn into the narrative by the hypnotic sea-like rhythms of the sentences. They listened for a full forty minutes, without coughing, sniggering or fidgeting, time losing its meaning before the power of the story.

Eventually Mr Chamberdale motioned for Johnny to stop as he came to the end of a chapter. There was complete silence in the room. The Principal leant forward across his desk.

'What you have been listening to,' said Mr Chamberdale, 'is not simply a story. It is literature. And literature is any arrangement of words that can transport us, despite our own will to resist, to whatever place it fancies. I have always been an admirer of the writings of Archdeacon Murphy. It is a great pity that he is not so widely read today. Now tell me, Mr Coughlan, what is it that made you take this book out of the library?'

Johnny hesitated. Obviously, he wasn't going to go into the whole story, so he simply said, 'I saw it on the shelves, sir, and took it out because it was one of his books that I had never heard of. He's a relation of mine sir, I mean, an ancestor. I've tried to read him before but couldn't quite get the hang of the way he wrote. But I think I get it now sir. I'm definitely going to finish *this* book, Mr Chamberdale. Oh, I did manage to finish one of his books before; it was called *The Woman at the Wave-Mouth*.'

'Oh yes,' said Mr Chamberdale with approval, 'a very good book indeed. Well, young Coughlan, I must say, I'm quite impressed. Yes, you've fairly redeemed yourself after an eventful week.'

At that moment the bell rang for the break and the class broke up.

On his way out of the classroom somebody tapped Johnny on the shoulder. It was Blister O'Flynn. Blister's real name was Barry, but he'd got the nickname after shaving his head, which everybody had thought made it look like a blister. The shaven head and the nickname seemed to suit him, so he kept them both.

Blister, who was very tall and a bit on the plump side, was wearing his usual combat pants and black boots. Over this he was wearing a biker's leather jacket, underneath which was a green v-neck jumper, his only concession to the school uniform.

'Are we still on for the band rehearsal tomorrow? Remember, you said last week that we'd get The Dead Crocodiles together on the first day of the May bank holiday. I hope it's not cancelled, 'cos we haven't met for ages and I'm worried we might be getting rusty.'

'God, Blister,' said Johnny, slapping himself on the forehead, 'I'd completely forgotten. Me and the lads had something planned ... but, you know, I think you're right, we haven't met in a while. Come down to Earc Luachra in the morning, about half-ten. We'll meet you at Snots's place, in the garage. We can gig for a while and then you can hang out with us. We've got some stuff to do, but you can tag along if you like.'

'Right,' said Blister. 'See you tomorrow, then.'

Johnny broke the news to the others in the yard.

'There's been a change of plan. Remember The Dead Crocodiles rehearsal we talked about last week? Blister just reminded me; I'd forgotten about it. I've told him to meet us at your garage, Snots, at half-ten. And I said he could hang out with us afterwards. Blister's sound. We'll explain everything to him, on a need-to-know basis. We'll just see how it goes.'

Nobody seemed put out that Blister was going to be there. Although he didn't normally pal around with them outside the band, they all got on well and he was quite adaptable, in the sense that when he was with them he was used to expecting the unexpected. And tomorrow that's what he'd probably get.

At that moment Jerry joined them and they began to finalise their plans for the weekend. As they talked they strolled over to the outbuildings behind the school, where they saw Monkey leaning against a wall, smoking a cigarette.

'Will you look at the eejit,' said Jerry, 'he thinks he's such a tough man. An ant would knock him down with a sneeze.'

Just then the bell sounded and Jerry and the gang went their separate ways back to class.

After the break Mrs Dooley took over from Mr Chamberdale. When they were all seated, she explained that Mr Chamberdale had some paperwork for the Department of Education that he had to finish before they broke up for the holiday. (What nobody knew was that the paperwork had come to a standstill. At that very moment Mr Chamberdale was preoccupied; he was examining something held tightly in the grip of his tweezers. It was one of his warts, and it had fallen from his face and on to his desk as soon as he had sat down.)

But now Mrs Dooley had charge of the class. 'Well, everybody, I hope you've all recovered after our little adventure the other day,' she said. 'Mr Chamberdale told me that he'd explained to you that it was just one of those things that happens from time to time and really meant nothing at all. What a silly-billy I was to make such a fuss.'

Jimmy Pats was looking at Mrs Dooley while she spoke. He knew she was talking a load of rubbish, and he knew that she was doing it on purpose, but he was

still in love with her. He reasoned that she was only doing it so that the class would put the whole matter behind them and wouldn't be worried by it, and he was okay with that kind of thing. Adults did it all the time and didn't seem to notice that they were fooling nobody. One day, when he had more time, he was going to make a study of this kind of behaviour, but not for the moment.

'Now, class,' said Mrs Dooley, 'as it's the last lesson before the holiday, I've decided that we're not going to do anything taxing; we're just going to de-stress, relax all those brain-muscles that we've been using all week. So, I want you all to get out your pencils and crayons, or colouring pencils or whatever, and I'm going to come round with some drawing paper. For the next hour I want everybody to just draw their favourite thing.'

Monkey, whose brain-muscles were as relaxed as you can get, put up his hand. 'Sorry, Miss, I don't know what to draw, Miss.'

'Then draw yourself,' said Mrs Dooley. 'Do a self-portrait.'

Monkey sat there, puzzled. He wasn't exactly sure what he looked like, and didn't know where to begin.

Jimmy Pats, on the other hand, had already started. He was drawing a picture of Mrs Dooley. Every now and then he'd look up at her in order to check a detail. He wanted his picture to be exactly right. He was going to pin it up above his bed.

Snots was drawing a blancmange. Blancmange was his favourite food and his favourite word, and therefore qualified to be drawn.

Orla Daly wanted to draw chewing-gum, but found it impossible to do.

Johnny drew a picture of Enya. In his picture she was wearing a white dress with tiny blue flowers and blue shoes. Normally she wouldn't be seen dead in such an outfit, but Johnny was simply feeling expressive. He drew a yellow flower in her right hand, but it didn't look quite right, so he rubbed it out and replaced it with a screwdriver.

Enya drew a picture of her crocodile, Gristle Bonehead. Above it she wrote the word MISSING in capitals. She could use it as a poster if he didn't turn up soon. The thought made her feel sad, so she turned the paper over and started to draw a picture of Johnny.

Blister O'Flynn drew a picture of The Dead Crocodiles. There were three of them. Himself on bass, Jimmy Pats on lead guitar and Johnny on drums. They were all wearing T-shirts with a picture of a crocodile across the front and the words *Reptiles Kill*.

Mrs Dooley also drew a picture. It was done mainly with shaded pencil. It showed a darkened room, its windows shuttered, the table and two chairs at its centre almost indistinguishable within the gloom. And to the side of the picture, drawn with a flourish of yellow crayon, was a shaft of light.

The Dead Crocodiles would have a new song ...

Jimmy Pats joined the bus at the roundabout, having gone home first to collect some gear and his electric guitar. The band usually left all their other stuff, like spare amps and mikes, at Snots's garage, so it saved them lugging too much from place to place.

Jimmy Pats made immediately for the back of the bus, holding his guitar in front of him, his backpack bumping off the side bars of the seats as he passed, and occasionally making contact with one of the occupants.

Enya was leaning with her face against the window and Johnny was sitting next to her reading *Tunnels of the Moon*, totally engrossed in the story. Snots was on the final rows of the second leg of the baling-twine trousers that had been ordered by Jerry, his needles clicking away at a steady pace. Jerry was reading *Animal Farm* and as he was reading he was moving his lips. Jimmy Pats, who could actually read lips, stopped in the aisle for a moment to read Jerry's; he made out the words '*chasing him round and round a bonfire when he was suffering from a cough*' and then decided to sit down next to him, putting his guitar and baggage on the seat beside him next to the window.

Enya, who was totally wrecked, had nodded off in the time it had taken Jimmy Pats to find his seat. The psychic concentration she had expended on her voodoo doll had left her exhausted. She started to snore, with a subtle thrumming of the lips. Johnny put down his book and began to listen. The sound of her snoring brought to mind a bass-line, and he began to think of the next day's rehearsal with The Dead Crocodiles. It dawned on him that he hadn't produced any new material in a while, so he started to mimic the sound of Enya's snore. Yeah, it *would* make a perfect bass-line. He continued playing the sound with his lips, improvising upon it. Maybe if he got it right he might be able to make up some new lyrics to go with it. If he could do that, The Dead Crocodiles would have a new song, something new to rehearse.

Snots had finished the actual knitting and was now sewing in the elastic at the bottoms of the legs, as Jerry had ordered.

Jimmy Pats, meanwhile, was turned in his seat, reading Jerry's lips from the side. He could make out the words '*the enemy both external and internal has been*

205

defeated' and decided that he would ask Jerry for a loan of the book once he'd finished with it.

After a few minutes Johnny no longer had to make the tune with his lips, for it was now thoroughly lodged in his mind. Enya, however, was still snoring the same tune, unknowingly accompanying him as he attemped to lay down some lyrics. He looked at her face and her long, slim fingers. Her hands had pronounced veins, and were very strong. She had lean but muscled arms. He remembered how she had dug the grave for the badger, how it wasn't a bother to her, and he felt puny next to her. Suddenly he was filled with a feeling of nervousness, some idea of inevitability that his mind could not articulate but his body could feel: he was suddenly terrified that she would find another boyfriend, somebody as strong as herself, somebody equally fearless. The bass-line resounding inside his head now filled him with an almost unendurable depression.

Jerry had become aware that Jimmy Pats was staring at him. He decided that he'd get to the end of the next sentence and then put the book away in his bag. He really hated it when people stared at him, especially if he was reading. Jerry stopped three-quarters of the way through a paragraph. Jimmy Pats was happily reading Jerry's lips, not realising that this was going to be the final sentence: '*He took his meals alone, with two dogs to wait upon him, and always ate from the Crown*

Derby dinner service which had been in the glass cupboard in the drawing-room.'

Jerry put the book into his bag.

Jimmy Pats was miffed. 'What did you stop reading for?' he asked. 'I was really getting into the story.'

'What story?' asked Jerry.

'In the book. I was reading your lips as you were reading the book. It's something I do. Comes in handy if I've forgotten to bring something to read.'

'Reading somebody's lips while they're reading? Listen, Buster, what do you think I am, a public library? That'll cost you twenty cents. Cough it up.'

'Pog off,' said Jimmy Pats. 'Man, you've really got an attitude problem.'

Johnny was becoming increasingly aware, by the tone of their voices, that Jimmy Pats and Jerry were quickly escalating towards an argument.

'Hey, you two plonkers,' he said, 'keep it down, will you! Enya's asleep, and she won't be too pleased if you wake her.'

Just in time to defuse the argument further, Snots finished making Jerry's baling-twine trousers.

'Finished!' Snots held up the completed trousers triumphantly. 'Try them on and see how they fit. I can make adjustments if there's anything wrong.'

Jerry lifted the trousers by the waistband and, standing up, held them against his legs. The length looked just about right. Then he climbed into them,

207

putting them over the pants he was wearing. He got both ends of the boot-lace belt and tied them as tightly as he could, with a double bow at the top. He began to walk up and down the aisle of the bus, and found that he could do so with ease because Snots had incorporated an innovation into this latest design. By changing the type of stitch directly at the back of the knee, the trousers now had a kind of hinge-effect, which made them flexible enough for the wearer to bend his legs.

Jerry looked down at himself. To the others the orange baling-twine trousers looked completely ridiculous, but Jerry, for reasons of his own, was delighted with the result. He went immediately to his jacket and got out the six euro he'd promised Snots and handed them over.

'Do you mind me asking, Jerry, but what do you want those things for?' asked Jimmy Pats, examining Snots's stitching close-up.

'For covering my legs while I walk,' said Jerry, which wasn't an explanation at all, when you think about it. But he wasn't prepared to elaborate.

Enya stirred and woke up. She seemed ratty, so Johnny decided not to start a conversation. However, after a minute of silence he relented.

'Are you okay?' he asked.

Enya didn't answer but simply leaned her face once more against the window. As he looked at her, he realised that her spots really were much better. Tying rags to trees and lighting thirty-three candles at a time obviously made a difference, after all. He began to wonder if Mr Chamberdale would be getting a new complexion.

'Listen, Johnny,' said Enya, almost as if she could read his mind, 'I don't want to light any candles today, so I'm not getting out at the church. I want to go straight to the Pits. I want to see them again. Will you come with me?'

'Yeah,' he said. 'We'll go to the Pits together. No problem.'

the creature in the rushes ...

The bus eventually came into Earc Luachra and they got off. Jimmy Pats was very excited at the prospect of seeing the shafts of light lying in the Pits.

But they weren't the only visitors that day. In the distance, standing on the very lip of one of the Pits, leaning against her bicycle, was the unmistakable figure of Peggy Delaney.

'What the hell is *she* doing up there?' asked Johnny, and then wondered why he should be surprised. Hadn't she been involved in this thing, one way or the other, from when it all started?

This time the ascent to the Pits was a marathon struggle, far worse than the previous time. The force field, or whatever it was that was trying to keep them away, was very strong. Their bodies felt as though they were made of stiffening toffee, as if at each step they were solidifying into some new, immovable substance.

'Jeeze!' said Jimmy Pats, 'you didn't say it was as hard as *this*.'

'It wasn't,' said Johnny 'It's like ... like ... they've installed some kind of new security device into the hill.'

'Yeah,' said Snots. 'It could actually *be* that. Maybe our first visit freaked them out.'

'So,' said Jimmy Pats, 'how did that old woman get up there? Look, she's running around the place like a two-year-old.'

'That's Peggy Delaney,' said Johnny. 'She's a friend of Snots, and isn't too bad, really, once you get to know her. She's the one that Chamberdale was talking about. Remember, the one who got us off the hook during detention today by telling him how impressed with us she was.'

'Oh,' said Jimmy Pats. 'But hang on a second, how

the hell did she *cycle* up this hill? I mean, for crying out loud, Johnny, look at the ground! We can hardly *walk* on it. There's no way even *we* could ride our bikes up here, and she's a fat old lady! It just doesn't make sense.'

'Watch yourself, there, Jimmy Pats,' panted Snots. He had exerted himself trying to catch up with them, and his breath was extremely laboured. 'I wouldn't insult her in her hearing if I was you. Peggy is a witch. I mean, a real one.'

'Man,' said Jerry. '*Now* he tells us!'

And in his mind Johnny was thinking: *Well, that explains a lot.*

When they got to the top, Peggy was waiting for them. 'So,' she said, eyeing them all up and down, 'I hear one of you was throwing stones into the water.'

'Nah, not us, Peggy,' said Snots.

'It was me,' said Enya, defiantly.

They were all taken by surprise.

'And when did you do this?' Johnny asked.

'This morning, when I came up here on my own. Remember, I already told you about coming up here. They'd just made me angry, that's all. I mean, they've been attacking everybody and driving them nuts. And they killed all those hedgehogs and badgers. And it's *my* crocodile that's gone missing. I take that personally. They *deserve* to have stones thrown at them, *whatever* they are. They don't scare me one bit.'

'Well, they *shouldn't* scare you, lovey,' said Peggy. 'They're only children, after all – even younger than yourselves.'

Everybody went: 'Uhhh?'

'They're the children of the Glimmer, so they are,' said Peggy. Then everybody noticed that she seemed to be throwing something into the Pits, but they couldn't quite see anything leaving her hands, even though they were all close to her. She was sweeping her right arm, and then her left arm, alternately, in a kind of flinging action, each time in the direction of the water in the three pits. The kids began to watch carefully. At first it was hard to make out exactly what was going on, but after a while they saw what was happening.

As Peggy threw her hands at the water, swarms of the tiniest insects, midges and dance-flies would accelerate through the air in the direction of her sweeping arms. There were thousands of them, thick, heavy clouds of them, dive-bombing towards the waters in the Pits and then sweeping up again. As soon as they came up they'd fall out of their cloud-like formations and settle into the ground, hidden in the grasses, until Peggy would sweep her arms again and back up they would come, moving through the air in a volley, then plummeting once more towards the water. As they swarmed down into the water, the wafers of light resting on its surface would part to let them move into the midst of them. And their miniscule wings would momentarily dazzle with a glittering of light.

'She's charming the midges,' explained Snots, 'just like the way I charmed the beetles the other day.'

'What is Snots talking about?' asked Jimmy Pats.

'You had to be there, Jimmy; it's something him and Peggy can do with insects. They can kinda control them. He showed us a day or two ago,' said Johnny.

'I could show you and Jerry tomorrow,' offered Snots, 'when we go to get Gristle from Tip Lake.'

Enya was speaking to Peggy Delaney. Seeing them together, Johnny was struck by how alike they seemed. Not that they looked anything remotely like each other, of course. But there was just a *feeling*, as though the two of them were on the same wavelength, shared an understanding that the others didn't.

'But what's with the midges, Peggy? What are you *doing*?' asked Enya.

'Oh, I'm playing with the Glimmer's children, lovey,' said Peggy, looking directly into Enya's face with her wild boss-eyes. 'Young children love to be played with and teased, and the midges hardly know that they're at it, their brains are so small. So they don't mind being a toy for the Glimmer's children, oh no they don't.'

'Hang on, Peggy,' said Johnny, 'what's a Glimmer? You've lost me completely.'

'The Glimmer, young fella, is the creature that lives in Earc Luachra. Actually, that's how the place got its name; the Irish words *earc luachra* mean: 'the creature in the rushes'. And the creature was the Glimmer. But because of the shape of the place, looking like a lizard, and because *earc luachra* is also the Irish name for lizards, people got all mixed up and they forgot about the Glimmer. There's been a Glimmer here since the beginning of time, but people can't see the Glimmer these days, they've forgotten how, so they have.'

'And you mentioned children, the Glimmer's children?' Jimmy Pats was careful to keep any doubt out of his voice, After all, as a scientist, he should be prepared to suspend judgement until he had heard the proof.

'Ah yes,' said Peggy, 'the children. About every hundred years or so, sometimes less, sometimes more, the Glimmer does have children. The last time it had young 'uns were in the days of your grandparents, in the early nineteen-twenties it was. And it wasn't any old lizard that Saint Fursa met, all those centuries ago; it was the Glimmer. According to my people, Saint Fursa and the Glimmer never fought. That's only a legend. But it's a legend that had its beginnings in truth. For, when Fursa first met the Glimmer, he mistook her for the devil. But they made friends after that, so never mind what the people in the Church say, or what's painted on the glass in the church window.'

Jimmy Pats and Snots had got their notebooks out and were writing down what Peggy was saying, like two dutiful reporters.

Jerry looked at them as if they were stone mad. 'Am I the only one here who's stopped hallucinating, or what?'

Peggy began to laugh. 'This young whelp is sharper than the lot of ye,' she said, looking at Jerry with unbridled admiration – sarcasm was something that she could appreciate, just so long as it wasn't directed at her.

'Never mind him,' said Enya. Looking at the two with their notebooks, she added, 'or those two eejits either. The thing is, you're talking about this Glimmer as if it's a pussy cat. But it's been messing with everybody's mind and has killed all the hedgehogs and badgers in the parish! The thing's a dangerous monster!'

'No,' said Peggy. 'No! There's no danger from the Glimmer. The Glimmer's just a mother who's given birth to its children and is now minding them till they're strong enough to leave her side. And the Glimmer didn't kill any hedgehogs or badgers, neither. All it did to the hedgehogs and the badgers was to disturb their signals – they're very sensitive, you know – which sent them into a confusion, just like it does to people. Before there were motor-cars in the world, the hedgehogs and the badgers would just go around

aimlessly for a while but then they'd recover and go back to their own ways. But that changed with the roads and all those contraptions speeding about, as though they can make extra time, when we all know that there's only the same amount of time as there always was. So it's the fault of men and their infernal motor-cars that the animals died. And the Glimmer never harmed no dogs either, they've just gone a-wandering, that's all. They'll be back in a day or two, when the fever of the Glimmer leaves them.'

'And what about my crocodile?' said Enya. 'Has *he* gone a-wandering too? 'Cos that could be a lot more serious than a few old dogs.'

Peggy laughed. 'Ah, that thing belongs to you, does it? I should have known. Well, he's quite safe, so he is. But you couldn't say the same for anything that's got in his way. He's eaten more dogs than the cars have killed badgers.'

'What, you actually know where he is?' said Enya, her mouth half-open in amazement and relief.

'Of course I do, lovey. He's down at the far end of Tip Lake, living next door to the Glimmer herself. Being a reptile, he's got an ancient kind of mind, so he has, so when he got the scent of the Glimmer he knew he only needed follow it to find all kinds of dazed animals in his path. You see, crocking-diles have the old forgotten knowledge that tells them the place of the Glimmer is the place to find easy food.'

'Hold it, hold it, hold it,' said Johnny. 'Look, you keep telling us what the Glimmer does, but you haven't actually said what the Glimmer *is*! Does it have a purpose, and if it does, what is it? I mean, how come we can't see it? And why exactly does it send people and animals round the bend?'

'The Glimmer is a creature,' said Peggy. 'The best way to describe its purpose is to say that it's a guardian, a kind of watchdog. It guards special places, where the realms of the normal world, that's the world that you live in, join up close to the realms of the spirit world. If there was no Glimmer to guard over the joins between the two realms, they'd both leak into each other and there'd be chaos.'

Peggy paused, folding her arms, the talons on her thumbs hidden in the folds of her baling-twine vest. 'Every country in the world has creatures the same as our Glimmer, but they call them by different names. In Australia, I believe, it's called a Bunyip, and in other parts of Ireland the Glimmer is known as the Pooka. They're more an animal of spirit than flesh and blood, so mostly people don't even know they're there. It's only when the babies come that people notice something strange. I was a young 'un, smaller than you, when this last happened here. My own mother brought me out to the waters round about, to see where the babies were. *Showing me the fairies*, she said she was. That's what the old people thought they

217

were, and, sure, maybe they were right, too. And for the two weeks that the babies are growing they behave like all babies, getting in everyone's way, and wanting to know the *why* of everything. Although you've only seen them during the day, the truth is they never stop. At night they flit over the hills, or occasionally high up into the sky, descending down like shooting stars. They have a way of getting into the minds of the other creatures they meet, although it affects people differently – I heard what happened to your Mr McCluskey. Some they make wise and some they make foolish. And they have a special fondness for children, being children themselves, but they don't take so well to most. They've taken well to you, though. Been attending your school, so I hear.' Peggy began to laugh. A gentle, good-natured chuckle.

'Hang on,' said Johnny, looking down into the Pits. 'There must be thousands of the things here. When they grow up, there'll be Glimmers *everywhere*.'

Peggy stopped laughing. A look came on her face, a sad look.

'Ah no,' said Peggy. 'The thing about it is, they all will die. Most are dying already. Another few days and you'll see them beginning to rot, dissolving into the skies. Before the week is out, they will all be gone. That's the way it is with Glimmers. That's why they have so many young. It's said, by those who pass down the knowledge, that only one single young Glimmer will live into adulthood every hundred-thousand years. They're not like the ants that swarm. No, Glimmers are different. The mother makes many, many Glimmers before the right one is made. Only then will the old mother die, and the new Glimmer take over. Only once every hundred-thousand years. And in the meantime the knowledge is passed down to people like me, and those of my kind. We are the servants of the Glimmer, simply rejoicing in her wonderful presence.' Peggy became quiet, her face thoughtful.

'But what about all that UFO stuff?' asked Jimmy Pats. 'And we saw police cars that *weren't there*. Everybody's seen them! What's *that* got to do with all of this?'

'Well now, me smart little man with your notebook, I'd say you've half-figured some of it out already. You see, this is the way it is: the Glimmer's children get into men's minds, but so does the Glimmer herself. She sends men and women and children off chasing wild ideas, and that way they're too busy to bother the Glimmer and her little ones. Although her young are dying, she wishes them to die in their own glories, not pestered and captured by people. The Glimmer goes inside your mind and finds out what's there, and then she uses that to suit her needs. Eighty years ago people believed in angels, so she made sure they saw angels. Today people don't believe in angels so much, but they believe in other things, like UFOs. So she makes them see UFOs. She can make herds of wild horses appear, or fill the streets with cars and lorries. Whatever she imagines will take shape and she can send them round and round for people to see. While the people are busy watching her visions in one place, she's safely nursing her children in another. Her compassion for her young is as sure as their deaths.'

'But, Peggy,' asked Snots, 'what kind of a creature is she? I mean, she's obviously very powerful, but the thing is, is the Glimmer good or evil?'

'Yeah,' said Enya, 'that's what *I* want to know too.'

Peggy looked at them all soberly. 'She's no more good nor evil than you are. She's just a creature about her business. She may be older than you are and more powerful, but she's still just a creature about her business. And her business is to guard the realms between the two worlds. Who's to judge if that's good or bad?'

Peggy began to lift her bicycle out of the grass. 'Well, it's time for me to be off. I'm running late. I'm off to the church to light a candle, and to say some prayers for the Glimmer and her children. Be sure to behave yourselves, now, when ye go after that crocking-dile of yours. Oh, and a word to you, Enya Murphy: if you wish to gain magic in the future, then I'd advise you not to steal it. Call on me and I'll teach it to you. Magic is for learning, not stealing. And you have the makings of someone who could learn.'

Peggy set off on the bike, travelling impossibly fast over the hilly grass. Johnny couldn't be sure, but as he watched her go he could have sworn that the wheels of her bicycle hadn't turned one single time.

They all looked down into the Pits. Enya picked up a stone, a heavy, jagged lump of a thing. And turning back, she threw it with all her might as far away from the Pits as she could, until it landed with a thump in the grass at the foot of the slope. She bent down and picked another stone and did the same. 'Do as I'm doing,' she said. 'We'll make sure that no one will trouble the Glimmer's babies with stones ever again.'

Soon they were all following her lead, until the lip at the edge of the Pits was free of stones.

On the way back down from the Pits no one needed to link arms as they had done the evening before. There was no fear or hesitation, which, after all, are only feelings that people get when faced with the unknown. As the gang walked back to Saint Fursa Estate, they could see shafts of light from the corner of their eyes, glimmering, glimmering.

They returned to the Pits later that evening, just as night was falling. They wanted to be there when the Glimmer's children swarmed from the Pits for their nightly wanderings. They wanted to be there for that moment. The walk to the top had been easy this time.

All of a sudden the Pits erupted with wafers of light

which burst over the three rims. The fields were bathed in a glorious second of daytime, and then the gang were left in darkness. Behind them, the Pits were gloomy hollows.

Then they made their way back down the slope for the second time that day – the third time for Enya. Ahead of them the house lights of the estate beckoned them home.

Jimmy Pats stayed with Snots, sleeping in the spare room. That night they all slept in their various rooms with the lights out. Shafts of light moved freely about their houses, passing into windows and through opened doors. None of them had trouble falling asleep or staying asleep. Their dreams were inhabited by the Glimmer's children, who moved through the darkness like the purest of lights.

SATURDAY

song for the disappointed ...

Johnny woke the following morning feeling brighter and more clear-headed than he had for a long time. He walked to the window and looked out at the sky. There was hardly a cloud to be seen. It was one of those May mornings when the sky is vibrant. He had a shower and got dressed. There was a lot to do. Today was going to be a day for crocodiles. First they were seeing Blister, who was coming down on an early bus for the band rehearsal. Then they'd be off to Tip Lake to locate Gristle Bonehead. Johnny wasn't sure how they would manage to bring him home, or even if they could. But he wasn't going to worry about it just yet.

Today required some appropriate clothing. He pulled on a pair of jeans and a cream T-shirt with cut-off sleeves. Enya had made the T-shirt for him; it had a black crocodile emblazoned across the front. Above the figure was the name of Johnny's band: The Dead Crocodiles.

Jerry was already sitting at the table before him and had prepared breakfast. Johnny looked down at his place-setting. The Teenage Ninja Mutant Turtles were floundering inside a bowlful of Frosties and cold milk. Johnny looked up to see Jerry looking at him.

'They're in the wastes of the Arctic Ocean,' explained Jerry. 'They've got caught on a melting ice-floe.'

Johnny decided to have toast.

After his breakfast he sat down near the living-room window and gazed out at the sky. The bass-line that he had got from Enya's snoring was running through his mind. He was thinking also of the Glimmer's dying children. And about his fear of losing Enya as his girlfriend. Everything was kind of getting mixed up inside his mind.

With the beat of the bass-line still running through his head, he rummaged for a biro and a sheet of paper and began to write. It was a poem. It was the new lyric for The Dead Crocodiles. He decided to call it 'Song for the Disappointed', and it wasn't like anything he had ever written before. It was as if there had been a change in him. There had.

At about half-past ten he and Jerry started out for the Saint Fursa Estate. They were running late, and by the time they arrived at Snots's house, answered the couple of questions that Mrs Murphy always asked, and were finally allowed through to the back garage, Blister had already arrived and was setting up his bass.

'Here, Blister, I've got a new bass-line I want you to try,' Johnny announced.

Johnny began thrumming the bass-line with his lips, and Blister soon picked it up, transferring it through his fingers to his guitar.

'Neat,' said Blister, approvingly. He began to play about with it, improvising, manipulating it until it sounded just right. He was a pretty tasty bass guitarist. Unfortunately, he was also the lead vocalist and the same couldn't be said of his voice.

Johnny let him at it for a few minutes, talking to Snots and Jimmy Pats. He wanted to give Blister some time to get comfortable with the bass-line first before giving him the new lyrics.

Snots set up the mike while Jimmy Pats was tuning his guitar. Over the months Jimmy Pats's playing had got a lot better, but he was still undoubtedly the worst guitarist in the world. No one could touch him.

Johnny checked out his drum kit, picked up his sticks and threaded them through the belt of his jeans.

'Hey, Blister,' said Johnny, 'check this out. It's the lyric to go with the new bass-line.'

Blister let his guitar hang loosely by its strap and took the piece of paper from Johnny. He read it several times, his head bobbing to an imaginary beat.

'This is pretty heavy, Johnny. Not like your normal stuff. But I like it. When did you write this one?'

'Just now,' said Johnny, 'after my breakfast. I've marked the breakdown of the beats over each of the words.'

'Yeah, I see that,' said Blister. 'Here, I'll give it a try, solo, just to get the hang of it, and then we can do it a few times together, with you and Jimmy Pats overlaying drum and lead guitar.'

Blister started to pick out the line with his guitar, and then, reading the lyrics from the paper which he'd placed at eye-level on a music stand, he began to sing.

As soon as the words started to come from Blister's mouth, Snots and Jimmy Pats looked up. They were gobsmacked. They had never heard lyrics like these before, but what was even more amazing was the way Blister was singing them. Blister, singing. *Really* singing. It was something to do with the lyrics. They had brought about a change in Blister. And they were now about to bring a change in the band.

'Way to go, Blister,' said Snots. 'Man, that was massive singing.'

'Wicked lyrics,' said Jimmy Pats.

'Good man, Blister,' said Johnny, 'that was deadly. Now let's see if we can all do it together. Let's show the world that The Dead Crocodiles can kick arse.'

As Blister started the bass-line and Johnny began to keep time on the drums, Enya walked into the garage. She sat down astride an old rocking-horse that had never been thrown out and listened in silence.

At first Blister just kept it instrumental, so that Jimmy Pats could have some freedom with his lead guitar. Actually, freedom was the last thing that Jimmy Pats's lead guitar should have had. In fact, Jimmy Pats's lead guitar should have been locked up. He launched into a riff that could turn milk into butter, kill song birds in mid-flight, eliminate the gap separating Heaven from Hell, and give terminal migraine to the finest mind in the universe. After a few moments, however, Jimmy Pats was beginning to tone it down. It could still thicken a grown man's brain into yoghurt, but it wasn't quite as bad as before. Something in the bass-line had brought about a change in Jimmy Pats's awful playing. It was no longer awful, just plain bad. Then Blister began to sing.

> Leaves fall from the trees
> They drift to the ground
> Insects trouble them
> They rot where they lie
>
> *I have a broken heart, a broken heart, a broken heart*
> *Oh I have a broken heart*
>
> Thick with ice
> The lake never dreams
> Fish bang against the sky
> The lake will not wake up
>
> *I have a broken heart, a broken heart, a broken heart*
> *Oh I have a broken heart*

The grave has caught me
The earth is without mercy
I swallow stones
Begin my slow decay

I have a broken heart, a broken heart, a broken heart
Oh I have a broken heart.

Enya listened on the rocking horse, galloping through riffs of a maniac's guitar into a place where only rock'n'roll can take you.

When the song was over the band brought everything to a close, finishing with Jimmy Pats doing a dirge of ear-splitting feedback.

'Wow,' said Enya. 'What was that called?'

'"Song for the Disappointed",' said Johnny. 'I wrote it this morning. The bass-line came into my head when I heard you snoring on the bus yesterday.'

'Well,' said Enya, 'if that's the case, then you're going to have to credit me as co-writer on the CD.'

'Yeah,' said Johnny. 'You got it.'

After the rehearsal the lads packed away their gear and locked the garage. Johnny had to go and get Jerry. They agreed to meet at the Pits in half an hour, from where they'd set off to find Gristle Bonehead.

Enya walked along with Johnny. 'So, have you really got a broken heart?'

'Nah,' said Johnny, 'not yet, anyway.'

'Then I'll make sure you don't get one – ever,' she

said, and flicked him gently on the nose. He would have preferred a kiss, but, lacking a kiss, a flick on the nose wasn't that bad. It'd do for now.

the news about Monkey was a bit disturbing ...

They all congregated at the Pits and showed Blister the wafers of light. It took him a while before he could see them properly, but then he got the hang of it. Then they filled him in on the whole story. He was used to weird stuff happening around these guys, so he just took the whole thing at face value. He was only jealous that he'd missed out on most of the fun.

After bringing him up to date, they made their way down the slopes at the other side of the Pits and towards the shops and the village. Enya was wearing a pair of jeans that she had bleached herself, and a pair of high-laced bright blue Doc Marten boots. She had on a long-sleeved blouse, which was a rarity with Enya. It was white and was covered in bright blue flowers the same colour as the boots. Johnny had never seen

her wearing either the boots or the blouse before. But what made it more curious was the fact that the colour of the boots was the same as the colour of the shoes he had drawn her wearing in the picture he had done in Mrs Dooley's class the day before. And the pattern and colours of the blouse were exactly the same as the dress he had drawn her wearing. The coincidence startled him and he couldn't work out what it meant, or if, indeed, it meant anything. Sometimes coincidence was just coincidence. And sometimes it wasn't.

Enya had a small rucksack on her back and a length of heavy-duty rope wound across her left shoulder. The rope was for tying up Gristle if they found him.

Snots was carrying the most enormous rucksack you could imagine, and everyone was curious as to what was inside it. Johnny guessed that he must have brought a tent or something. Snots was wearing a tracksuit and baseball cap and was feeling really good today. He wanted this feeling to last. He hoped it would.

Jerry also had a rucksack, but a small one like Johnny's. Inside Jerry's was his baling-twine trousers, which he hoped to be able to try out during the course of the day.

Jimmy Pats travelled light. The only piece of equipment that he carried was his notebook and a biro.

As they came to the outer fringe of the village they passed the old Earc Luachra National School. Nowadays this was used mostly as a community centre but was still owned by the school in Kilfursa, who operated it as an annex whenever they needed to. In fact, only a few months ago it was opened for a week while the primary classrooms were being painted. Johnny and the gang had gone there to school and a bus had come down from Kilfursa every day with the Kilfursa kids and the three teachers, Mr McCluskey, Mrs Dooley and Miss Murphy-Rasheen. They had had great fun for the whole week until the school reverted back to Kilfursa once more. Enya had even brought Gristle to school one day and none of the teachers had noticed.

The gang finally got through the village and made their way to the shore of Tip Lake. They intended to take one of the rowboats belonging to Enya's Uncle Danny.

Waiting for them by the boat was Peggy Delaney, balancing on her bicycle.

'I thought I'd better tell ye,' she said. 'I was in the village just half an hour ago and I met someone who was enquiring after ye. He was burly-looking with spiked hair, and I didn't like him one bit. He'd come down from Kilfursa in the second bus. He told me he was looking for Jerry because he wanted to "*re-establish his business arrangement*". They were the

exact words he used. He also said something to the effect that there wasn't a single dog to be found in the whole of Kilfursa. Just thought you'd like to know.'

'Ah man,' said Johnny, 'it's that plonker, Monkey!'

Johnny watched very carefully as Peggy cycled off, and he was certain beyond any doubt that the wheels of her bicycle didn't turn once, though the bicycle itself shot off at tremendous speed.

Although the news about Monkey was a bit disturbing, especially to Jerry, there was nothing they could do about it right now, so they decided to unmoor the boat without delay and head across the water. The plan was to check along the length of the lake, stopping off on Feeney Island in the centre, and then on to Rushy Island at the far end of the lake. Rushy Island was a sedgy, arrowhead-shaped lump of marshy land surrounded by reed-clogged water. They slipped the boat from its ties and rowed out, Blister and Enya taking the oars first, for they were the strongest.

They were an hour out from the shore, and Johnny and Jimmy Pats were taking their turn at the oars, when Jerry called out that he could see something in the water towards Feeney Island. The island was about fifteen minutes off, and Snots opened the pocket at the front of his rucksack and brought out a pair of binoculars.

'It's a dog,' he said, 'swimming through the water.

Actually, I can see dozens of them, all going towards the land.'

Jerry, who didn't really like dogs, began to get uneasy.

Snots re-focused the lens so that he could see the island itself.

'So that's where they all went to,' he said. 'The island is full of dogs. They're just lying down. Looks like they're all napping. The only ones moving seem to be the ones in the water.'

At the news that most of the dogs were asleep, Jerry began to relax. The cogs in his cunning brain began to turn faster. He started to wonder if perhaps his plan to locate Mr Chamberdale's dog, Vigrid, could be made operational, after all. That'd be forty euro – the highest reward. Not bad. Pity he couldn't manage all the other dogs: he'd totted up the reward money offered all around the village for the safe return of the dogs. It was more than he'd ever dreamed of – yet. But he decided he'd focus on Vigrid. He'd be able to manage that. He'd have lots of help from the gang, so he would not be requiring the services of Monkey, after all.

As they got to the nearest shore of Feeney Island, the water around them was full of dogs, swimming about steadily. They looked a bit dazed, but seemed quite happy in a doggy sort of way. This made Jerry feel even more at ease.

They eventually landed on the island and tied the boat securely to a tree. There were dogs everywhere, most of them just lying down passively, many of them fast asleep. Snots and Jimmy Pats went amongst them, checking their heartbeats and stuff like that. They had plenty to enter into their notebooks.

'Their heartbeats seem to be quite slow,' said Jimmy Pats, 'as if their metabolisms have gone into a lower gear. But they seem all right. The only thing is, they're an easy meal for Enya's crocodile.'

'Yeah,' said Enya, not feeling much sympathy for the dogs, 'but he needs to eat *something*. I mean, he's a crocodile, so what can you expect? And he can't eat *all* of them. There'll still be plenty of dogs left.'

Jerry was praying that Gristle hadn't eaten Vigrid.

'There's no need to be defensive, Enya,' said Johnny. 'Jimmy Pats wasn't trying to have a go at you, he was just making an observation.'

Snots had a suggestion. 'I reckon we should split up into two groups and search the island for any signs of Gristle's presence. We'll meet up here in exactly an hour.'

'Good idea,' said Jerry. 'And look out for Vigrid while you're at it.'

Jerry, Blister and Snots went off along the western side of the island and Johnny, Enya and Jimmy Pats searched the eastern side. They hadn't gone their separate ways long when a tremendous yelping started up somewhere in the centre of the island.

An hour later they met back at the boat and Snots reported how they had seen Gristle leave the island with a dead poodle in its mouth. He had slipped into the water and was headed towards the far end of the lake, in the direction of Rushy Island.

There was also some good news for Jerry. Blister had found Vigrid, fast asleep close to the shore. So they got Vigrid, as soundly asleep as Murphy, into the boat and took off in pursuit of Gristle.

Jerry sat some distance from the sleeping dog at first, but after a while he became lulled by the dog's regular breathing and moved closer. Vigrid didn't seem so intimidating, asleep in the bottom of the boat. Jerry began gradually to adjust his fear. His main problem now was to make sure *he* got control of Vigrid – so he'd get the reward for himself.

a walking maggoty worm-man ...

About forty minutes later, exhausted from rowing, and having lost sight of Gristle, they were near the boggy shore of Rushy. A strange glow hung over the whole island, turning the air a shade of bright green.

'This must be where that Glimmer hangs out,' said Blister.

'I think it *is* the Glimmer,' said Snots. 'I think it's so big that it's resting over this whole place. I suppose an isolated island like this is the best place for it to hide. But maybe this is unsuitable for its babies, and that's why it keeps them in the Pits. Look, I've brought some special gear, so I'm going on to the island. Enya and Jerry can come with me: Jerry, 'cos he's got a pair of baling-twine trousers in his bag. They'll protect his legs from the leeches. And I've got a spare pair for Enya, and a special suit for myself. I'm going to see if I can make contact with the Glimmer. I noticed that

Peggy did it with the Glimmer's babies by using insects. I'm going to try something similar with the Glimmer itself. I'm going to see if I can get it to help us locate Gristle. Then Enya can secure him with the rope.'

'This is great,' said Jerry. 'This is an even *better* use for those trousers. At first I wanted them to protect my legs from being bitten by the dogs. But when Monkey pulled out of the deal and it looked like I wasn't going to be able to go dog-hunting, I then decided to see if they were good protection against furze bushes. Once on the islands I thought I could walk through the furze and collect wild bird's eggs. There's lots of money to be had in wild bird's eggs.'

'It's also highly illegal,' said Johnny, 'not to mention a possible magnet for bad karma.'

Enya had to take off her Docs to put her baling-twine trousers on, but once she had the boots back on, the elasticated legs gripped around the ankles quite securely.

While she was getting dressed, Snots put on his own strange outfit: a baling-twine boiler suit with baling-twine boots. He also had a baling-twine balaclava with holes for his eyes and a looser woven grille for his mouth. When he had it on it looked a bit like an old-fashioned diving-suit, except that it wouldn't have been much use under water. Then he put on a pair of goggles.

'Man, what the hell is that?' said Johnny, examining all the bits and pieces.

'This,' said Snots, 'is my own invention. It's an Insulation Mantle-Suit for the transportation of creepy crawlies.'

'If you say so,' said Johnny.

'You'll see when I start to do my charming thing. Now, Jerry and Enya, whatever happens, I want you to stay behind me. Don't get worried if there's some weird stuff going on – I expect that. Just keep an eye out for Gristle. If you get a chance, put the rope around him. Now, follow me.'

As they walked along through the boggy ground, Snots started to make strange noises, squeeky, belchy kinds of noises. Worms, leeches, maggots and beetles began to writhe out of the ground and make their way up the legs of Snots's suit. He was totally insulated from them, as they couldn't get inside, but within minutes he was covered completely, a walking, maggoty worm-man. Jerry and Enya looked at each other in bewilderment.

He signalled to them to stay where they were. Then, when he and all his maggoty worms got to the centre of the island, he stopped walking and stood perfectly still. He called over to Enya and Jerry.

'Stand still and don't talk. Do and say absolutely nothing until I tell you.'

This is what happened next.

The Glimmer, immense, invisible, incredibly ancient upon the earth, one of the great guardian spirits of places, was alerted to a sudden upsurge in creature-activity, and it was an upsurge that she knew *she* was not responsible for.

She lifted her wings and rose from Rushy Island, hovering over the boggy land. Enya and Jerry, and the others by the boat, were suddenly aware of a brightening in the air, as if very intense lightning was flashing constantly.

The Glimmer could see a man below her on the island, a man the likes of which she had never seen in all her centuries of existence. He was a maggoty worm-man, standing perfectly still. Behind him were two human children, obviously his servants.

The Glimmer, obliged to investigate, sent her mind down into the mind of the maggoty worm-man. There she found, to her surprise, the mind of Snots Murphy. It was a mind that delighted her. A good and clever mind. The mind of a small, constantly snotty-nosed boy, who nonetheless took what little he had and made it work for him. And here he was, a twelve-year-old human pupling, commanding the attention of one of the planet's ancient guardians. And his desires of the Glimmer were small. In order to help one of his friends he required the taming of a crocodile.

The Glimmer searched about and found the reptile

up to its neck in mud, grinding its teeth into a dead poodle. She stilled its tiny but ferocious brain, and sent it out as meek as a butterfly.

Enya and Jerry could see Gristle, completely covered in muck, waddling towards them. When he reached the feet of Snots he stopped and waited, perfectly still.

They watched as worms and maggots and leeches and beetles slithered away from the body of Snots, until all they could see was their twelve-year-old friend wearing a ridiculous suit made from orange baling twine.

Gristle was quite docile, so they looped the rope around his neck, and, just to be on the safe side, made a muzzle for those deadly jaws. After all, Jerry didn't want him eating Vigrid. Then, leading him like a baby on a walking-reins, they made their way back to the boat.

Snots sent a mental note of thanks up to the Glimmer, and it shone in the Glimmer's incredible mind no more brightly than a lighted match inside the sun. Soon, the Glimmer was lost once more in its contemplation of greater things. The force of its thought was wedged in the gap between the worlds.

Taking turns to row, they slowly crossed the lake, Gristle Bonehead swimming in the water behind them, tied securely to the boat with the rope. And at their feet was Vigrid, contentedly snoring.

That afternoon it was widely reported throughout the townland that the majority of the dogs had come home. Strangest of all was the phonecall reputedly received by Mr Chamberdale from a young pupil living all the way down in Earc Luachra. Apparently, the Principal's dog was spending the duration of the May holiday living in the pupil's house, sleeping in the pupil's bed and eating from the pupil's hand. Furthermore, the pupil respectfully requested the sum of forty euro, so promised on a note pinned to the school noticeboard, to be ready for his collection first thing at the resumption of school during the following week. The pupil also alluded to 'costs' which he said he would elaborate on as soon as he had an opportunity to work them out.

It was also reported that a crocodile, known to be the pet of a local girl, was seen walking through the village with a group of twelve-year-olds, the remains of a dead poodle lodged firmly between its grinning teeth. And there were those who said that a strange creature, composed entirely of orange baling twine and sporting a heavy stick, had been seen chasing another boy, a boy reported to be from Kilfursa town, a boy by the improbable name of Monkey Murphy. This boy had been seen running in fear from the baling-twine creature until he'd caught up with the afternoon bus that finally took him all the way home to Kilfursa.

Although some people doubted the truth of these stories, *The Ballynought Review* boldly carried a special

supplement, detailing the whole fantastic tapestry of reports, in their very next edition. There were even interviews with many elderly people who claimed that something not very dissimilar had happened in the townland in 1922.

It turned out to be one of the biggest-selling issues in the history of the paper.

he dropped the wart into an empty ink bottle ...

The school bus pulled into the kerb outside the school and the pupils poured off. With them was Jimmy Pats Murphy, who had spent a very interesting weekend with his buddies in Earc Luachra. Last to leave the bus was Jerry, who was leading Vigrid on a lead made from orange baling twine. Vigrid was also wearing a matching dog-coat, made from the very same versatile material.

In the playground Jerry and Vigrid were approached by Monkey, who changed his mind very quickly as soon as Vigrid began to growl at him, white saliva foaming at his mouth.

Jerry was going to be flush for the rest of the term. He was many euro the richer and his karma was swelling in the bank. On top of that, Vigrid, totally spoiled after the holiday in Earc Luachra, could safely be counted on to be a loyal bodyguard to the gang. No

more would they have to worry about the likes of Monkey Murphy.

Holding tightly to Vigrid's baling-twine lead, Jerry surveyed the school yard. Yes, one day he could very well rule the world.

Meanwhile, Mr Chamberdale was sitting at his desk with the tweezers firmly in his grasp. And in the grip of the tweezers was a wart, the fifth that had fallen from his face since last Friday. If this continued, his face would be clear of warts within seven months. He dropped the wart into an empty ink bottle, where it joined its four compatriots, and got up from his desk. Gazing from the window he looked down into the school yard and saw his dog, Vigrid, returned to him at last. He placed his hand inside his jacket pocket and removed an envelope. On it was written: *For Jerry Coughlan: 40 euro reward for return of dog, plus 40 euro to cover dog's bed and board for the duration of the May holiday, as agreed by 'phone. Total=80 euro. With Compliments, Mr C. Chamberdale.*

Mr McCluskey was busy writing on the blackboard. Ten sums, all multiplication, waiting impatiently to be solved. Mr McCluskey had obviously recovered from his bout of Oriental 'flu. The classroom was his to terrorise once more.

From the corner of his eye, Johnny could see tiny strands of light hanging from the ceiling. Even as he strained to look he could see them disintegrating, becoming increasingly unstable. They were rotting under the harsh, ordinary daylight. They were the only proof that something marvellous had happened in Kilfursa, and now they were nearly gone.

'*Coughlan!*' called McCluskey. 'What the blazes are you looking at, boy?'

'Eh ... nothing, sir,' said Johnny.

'Then I suggest you stop looking at nothing and start looking *at something*. The blackboard, Coughlan, *the blackboard. Look at the blackboard, boy!*'

Johnny looked at the blackboard. It was full of sums, columns upon columns of tiny numbers demanding to be made sense of.

'*Well*, Coughlan? Sum number one: perhaps you would be good enough to suggest an answer? Go on, Coughlan, *take your time*. After all, the lesson will last *a whole hour* ...'

Johnny could see that nothing had changed. He made a wish. Just a tiny one. He wished that Mr McCluskey would get off his back and pick on somebody else.

But there was no shooting star to wish by, and he knew now that wishes had a tendency to turn out bad. He was not invincible. He was Johnny Coughlan, Coffin to some – drummer, big brother and boyfriend. And today was just another day in school.

A Note from the Author

Dear Reader,

Although this is only my second Johnny Coffin book, I've been writing Johnny's adventures for my radio show 'The Ivory Tower', for over two-and-a-half years. In that time I have written 103 half-hour episodes. That amounts to over fifty hours of radio time, and when I finally get to translate all those stories on to the page it will give me another seven books.

Unfortunately, by the time I had finished writing my radio series my poor brain was like a badly fried egg: crispy on the outside and gungy in the middle. For this reason this book is a few months late, and to those of you who have been waiting for it, I apologise.

Since the first book came out, many of you have written me letters. It really is nice for an author when he hears from his readers. Being a writer can be lonely sometimes, because you're locked away in your room, making up all kinds of things to put inside your books and you have no idea if anyone will like them or not.

Lots of people have asked me where I get my ideas from. Well, to tell you the truth, I get them from Johnny Coffin. Johnny's stories are bits of mine, with some made-up things thrown in. But, all-in-all, Johnny Coffin and myself are the same person. And all that mad stuff that happens to Johnny, well, it all happened to me first. I'll give you an example. Do you remember the chapter about the budgie in *The Johnny Coffin Diaries*? Well, that started from something that really happened. When I was about twelve my Dad brought home a budgie which he had found at work on the

building site. The thing was, neither my Mum nor my Dad thought of getting a cage for the budgie for at least three weeks. The budgie used to perch on the lampshade in the living room and would fly freely about the house, leaving his droppings everywhere. Mum would go round later with a dustpan and brush, cleaning up his mess. I'd bring my friends in to see the budgie and they'd be surprised to find that it could be anywhere. Sometimes they'd go to the loo and there would be the budgie, sitting on the toilet, singing its twittering little song. When my parents finally got a cage for the budgie he just sat inside it and sulked. He never sang again, not in all the years that we had him. And that memory was the thing that helped me think up that chapter in *The Johnny Coffin Diaries*.

Inside this book you'll find many mad things. Some are more true than you could imagine. Some things in this book actually happened to me and some could never happen in a million years. But I'll leave it to you to argue over which is which.

Kenmare
July 2002

If you would like to send comments to John W Sexton
you may do so at: johnwsexton@obrien.ie
He would love to hear from you.

Acknowledgements

In 1966, at the age of eight, I read my first novel from start to finish. It was a hardback with a plain yellow cover and I had chosen it from the classroom library. I can't remember the author's name, but the book was a Lone Ranger adventure, and its opening sentence has stayed with me for over thirty-six years. Those first words said the following: 'The sun shone out of the sky like a bronze coin.'

Finishing that book was the hardest stretch of reading I'd done up until then. Before that I'd read nothing but comics. And the reason I mention it is because it was one of those works of fiction that got me started on this long road of writing. I don't remember the author's name, but I never forgot his opening sentence. It has stayed inside my head like a shard of glass shining in the dark.

The authors whose names I do remember from those days wrote nothing but comics. The greatest of them all, to my mind, was Jack Kirby. Jack Kirby was principally an artist, but he also wrote. Among his creations are Mr Miracle, The Forever People, Granny Goodness (who was evil beyond compare), Big Barda, The New Gods, Devil Dinosaur, Destroyer Duck and many more. In collaboration with Stan Lee he also helped to create The Fantastic Four, Dr Doom, Galactus and The Silver Surfer.

But my favourite comic of all was *The Green Lantern,* written by two jobbing science-fiction writers, John Broome and Gardner Fox. Reading through those monthly pages was like dreaming without having to fall asleep.

All those writers ignited the tinder in my imagination that demanded that I read more and more. And it wasn't long after I was alight with reading, that I wanted to write myself. And that's what I've been doing ever since. Putting these words at the end of my own

book is my way of saying thank you to those comic-book writers who set me scribbling.

I'd also like to thank Anthony McGuinness for naming the beast; Jack Doyle Ryan for his masterly interpretation of Johnny Coffin on radio; Seán Corcoran for being his inimitable self; the show's producer, Jacqui Corcoran, for keeping me writing even when I thought I couldn't go on; Margaret O'Shea for accompanying me oftentimes along the lonely road of poetry; and my dearest friend Eileen Sheehan for shining a light against that shard of glass.

Finally I must thank my editors at The O'Brien Press for patience bordering on saintliness.

What's on www.obrien.ie?

➤ detailed information on *all* O'Brien Press
books, both current and forthcoming

➤ sample chapters from many books

➤ author information

➤ book reviews by other readers

➤ authors writing about their own books

➤ teachers' and students' thoughts about
author visits to their schools

What are you waiting for?

Check out <u>www.obrien.ie</u> today.

ARE YOU READY TO RETURN TO THE WORLD OF JOHNNY COFFIN?

THE JOHNNY COFFIN DIARIES
John W Sexton

Meet Johnny Coffin: a school-hating, music-loving, hen-pecked young man with a habit of getting into all kinds of trouble. But then, only someone who loves trouble would go out with Enya, the craziest person in Johnny's school – and that's *really* saying something. Johnny's struggles with English literature and boring homework, with his manic teacher Mr McCluskey and the mad bunch of Murphys who occupy his classroom and, of course, with the attentions – good and bad – of his girlfriend, Enya, are all documented in his diary. It's the truth, the whole truth. No joking.

Paperback €6.95/stg£4.99/$7.95

ALSO FROM THE O'BRIEN PRESS

BENNY AND OMAR
Eoin Colfer

A hilarious book in which a young sporting fanatic is forced to leave his beloved Wexford, home of all his heroes, and move with his family to Tunisia! How will he survive in a place like this? Then he teams up with Omar, and a madcap friendship between the two boys leads to trouble, crazy escapades, a unique way of communicating, and heartbreaking challenges.

Paperback €6.95/stg£4.99/$7.95

BENNY AND BABE
Eoin Colfer

Benny is visiting his grandfather in the country for the summer holidays and finds his position as a 'townie' makes him the object of much teasing by the natives. Babe is the village tomboy, given serious respect by all the local tough guys. She runs a thriving business, rescuing the lost lures and flies of visiting fishermen and selling them at a tidy profit. Babe just might consider Benny as her business partner. But things become very complicated, and dangerous, when Furty Howlin also wants a slice of the action.

Paperback €6.95/stg£4.99/$7.95